NASCENT SHADOW

TEMPORAL ARMISTICE BOOK 1

MATTHEW S. COX

DIVISION ZERO PRESS

Nascent Shadow
Temporal Armistice Book 1

(c) 2017 Matthew S. Cox
All Rights Reserved

ISBN (ebook) : 978-1-949174-72-4

ISBN (print) : 978-1-949174-73-1

CONTENTS

1

BURNING PROBLEM

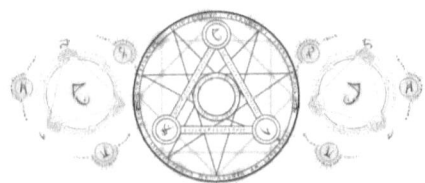

Unease haunts the back of my mind. It's always there waiting to ambush me. It pounces during the lulls of calm in idle moments, and savages my emotions when I try to sleep. Ever since I've been a little girl, leaving me alone in a quiet place has been a bad idea, so I tend to distract myself by doing weird things— like levitating my seventy-inch television while watching *Dead Like Me.*

I'm pissed it only lasted two seasons, but it's from 2003. I was only nine when it came out, and I didn't discover it until college, so it's not as if I could've done much about it being canceled. At least I've got it on DVD. Found the box set on a table at some flea market my friend Natalie insisted on going to. Who'd have thought spending four bucks would've been so cool? Unfortunately, my dorm mate wound up loathing the show since I played it constantly.

I had to keep my brain busy. Silence was my enemy.

From my first moment in the school system, I felt like I didn't fit in. The year I turned twelve, my mother's house burned down. That's when I *knew* I didn't fit in. No, I didn't cause the fire, but I almost died in it. In fact, I should have. No one could explain how I made it out, and I don't remember.

Those 'friend' things everyone keeps telling me about are overrated. I didn't resonate with any of the other kids in school, and now that I've been accused of being an adult, I jibe even less with people outside the framework of a job. Oh, sure, I can interact with them easily enough on a professional level, just not for fun. Kids, no problem. I can get along with them.

On a lazy Tuesday night like this, I often wind up in a half-tee and sweatpants, lying on my couch and making random things float around. It keeps my mind off that creeping unease that likes to remind me about what could go wrong. Besides, I'm too old to get into trouble now. No more slap on the wrist from the cops.

Let me walk that back a hair. I do have one friend—Natalie. Her bell rings at the same not-quite-in-tune-with-society frequency as mine. We met in college after my *Dead Like Me* hating roommate demanded a transfer. Natalie moved in and went past best friend into almost-sister pretty quick.

Overall though, most Tuesday nights wind up with me on the couch like this. Tonight's half-tee is violet, with a black and white anime girl in chibi style dressed like a grim reaper. I set the television back down on its stand, bored. So, yeah, I'm telekinetic. Born with it, but I didn't figure it out until a couple days after the fire. I mean, really. Whoever expects to be telekinetic? It's not the sort of thing that happens to people. And maybe some *Star Wars* junkies randomly try to use it, but none of them really expect it to work.

It's far more common for kids to develop magical abilities.

No such luck for me. Oh yay, I can move crap with my mind. Meh. Anyone who can wield magic attracts a cluster of gawkers. I'd much rather be left to my own devices, alone, at home, on a Tuesday night, making my TV fly around the room.

Really.

I sigh.

Maybe I should get a cat.

I move some chairs back and forth with my mind, spinning them as they glide by. A chair happened to be the first thing I ever affected with telekinesis. Said article of furniture belonged to my sixth-grade teacher, Mrs. Straczynzki. She wasn't necessarily a bad teacher, but she decided to take issue with my wearing the same dress four days in a row. After the fire, I had a pretty limited wardrobe for a while, and Mom couldn't afford to replace it. The other kids laughed at me, and when Straczynzki went to sit down, her chair flew into the wall out from under her.

When I realized she'd broken her hip, I stopped laughing… but I still smiled.

Screaming in the next apartment to my left seeps into my living room, loud enough to drown out Ellen Muth's existential crisis monologue. Did I mention my apartment is on the cheap side? Yeah. Thin walls. I think her name is Tracy. She's older than me, like almost thirty. Has a kid, too. A little brown-haired girl, but I'm not sure what her name is. Feel sorry for her havin' to listen to her mother and this month's asshole go three rounds every damn night. Tracy seems to have a different flavor of jackass every six weeks or thereabouts. Almost all of them like screaming. Maybe it's her that likes screaming and she rubs off on them. It's a little after nine, so I've probably got an hour before shouting advances to full-contact MMA.

I stretch out and put my heels up on the coffee table. Pale crescents on my toenails tell me it's time for another coat of black. I like my nails to match my hair, but I can't really paint my fingernails anymore. Not with the job. *Argh!* It drives me crazy that some prig behind a desk cares what color my nails are. Like some random dude I pull out of a building is gonna complain to the department 'oh, that woman who saved my life had color on her nails. That's not professional.' *Sigh.* I have this deep-seated need to paint them all black. It started around ten or so, and I used to have to shoplift nail polish. It's such a triviality, I couldn't ask my mother to waste money on it. But, I skip the fingernail decoration now. It's hard enough getting them to take me seriously as a woman, plus the job often gets dirty and rough. No point picking a useless fight. Despite it all, I love being a firefighter. I guess you could say it's my calling.

I've been drawn to it ever since my mother's house burned.

It happened eleven years ago, before Mom realized she had a little bit of magical talent and decided to try writing self-help books, or more accurately, how-to books for seers. At the time of the fire, she waited tables at a shithole of a greasy spoon that stayed open until two in the morning. You know what kind of babysitter a single mother can afford when they're working as a waitress? Mine was a small television and a whole bunch of hope that nothing bad happened before she came home.

Mom tells me I'd always been a handful. When I was tiny, it took her forever to get me to keep my clothes on. I'd climb everything I got near, open any door I could reach, try to eat anything that came close to my mouth. If I got it in my head that I wanted something, I would stop at nothing to get it, at least until the next random 'ooh, that looks cool' thought came along. I'm honestly surprised Mom didn't have multiple heart attacks.

Those news stories about a four-year-old found wandering naked two miles from their house? Yeah, that was me. Like six times.

Reports of a seven-year-old stealing their parent's car and driving to get ice cream? Yep. Me.

You hear the one about a nine-year-old girl in moon boots, a panda hat, and underpants riding a skateboard down the middle lane of the Pennsylvania Turnpike at oncoming traffic? Yep. Me.

I'd been picked up by the police more times before age thirteen than some career criminals, though I didn't technically get arrested until fourteen. Shoplifting. When I was little, they found me in places I didn't belong and took me home. Mom was always working. It ultimately took her begging me not to do crazy shit again because they'd take me away from her to get me to stop.

Back to that single-mother thing. I never knew my dad. Mom never talks about him. She gets all spacy and weird whenever anyone brings him up. I figured out pretty young that the man who fathered me probably raped my mother. There's no pictures of him anywhere. My mother's friends claim not to have known she'd been seeing anyone, and as a kid, I never found even *one* item belonging to a man in our home. Maybe she'll tell me about it someday, if she can ever get over the pain of what happened.

I love my mom. She's the kindest, sweetest, most patient person in the world. While I'm sure lots of kids think that about their parents, I know for a fact there isn't a single more patient person on the planet. My mom had to deal with *me* as a teenager, and she didn't kick me out, surrender me for adoption, or give up. No matter how many times she had to pick me up from the police station, she never lost her temper with me.

'Course, I never really did anything *that* bad. Shoplifting, graffiti, underage drinking, staying out past curfew, trespassing in condemned buildings, that sort of thing. I never stole anything someone else needed, did any real property damage, or hurt anyone. Never stole a car either, but more out of fear of punishment. I wanted to have fun, not do something that would ruin my life. What can I say? I have weak impulse control.

Okay, back that up. I did hurt that one guy who tried to lure me into a car when I was ten. I may have *looked* innocent, but the second I made eye contact with him, I knew exactly what he wanted to do to me. Let's just say it involved duct tape, a few hours of an activity no ten-year-old child should ever participate in, and ultimately, a shallow grave for yours truly. Rather than terrify me, I wound up getting highly pissed off.

I still don't entirely understand what happened. One second, I'm staring at him, wanting him to suffer the most painful, slow death a little kid can think of, and the next, there's a huge explosion of blood from his nose and he slumps over the wheel. That I didn't feel anything other than 'good, he needed to die' kinda freaked me out, but I kept it to myself.

When Mom's house caught fire two years later in 2006, I figured the universe had decided payback was in order. I can't remember every little detail of that night, and whenever I try to, my little anxiety goblin reminds me he's still sitting in the back of my mind. Mom had a singlewide near the back corner of a trailer park. The area had its problems: drugs, gangs, alcoholic assholes, untrained mages who practiced their magic on who or whatever they could. Anyone too poor to get into one of the academies had to work stuff out for themselves.

Anyway, after the perv in the car, I kinda wound up 'patrolling' my trailer park. I didn't care about the drugs or gangs; mostly, I wanted to make sure no more strange cars or vans came rolling around in search of poor children no one would miss. Fortunately, I never did need to 'nose-explode' anyone else.

On that particular night, however, I stayed home. It's been a while, and I half want to say it was raining, but no, now that I think about it, someone had complained to Mom about me roaming around past midnight and threatened to call the authorities on her. Pretty sure the 'Good Samaritan' didn't actually care about my welfare—they just didn't want some kid watching them turn tricks.

The trailer was tiny, and my room sat all the way at the back end. Mom had let me have the bigger room since she only used her bedroom for sleeping while I kinda lived in mine. I was sitting on the floor, engrossed in my PlayStation 2 (yeah, I stole it), when an explosion shook the trailer and fire went everywhere.

Like I said, the night's a bit of a blur. I remember staring into a wall of fire out in the hall and thinking I had nowhere to go, and the next thing I know, I'm walking over the grass out front. A cool breeze told me my pajamas were gone. To this day, I still can't remember how I wound up naked or got out of there. I figure a while passed between the fire starting and me appearing outside since my mom had been there, crying. It had to be at least six minutes—so she had time to drive home from work. As soon as she saw me, she went from sobbing to screaming, and a fireman had run over to collect me in a blanket.

Ever since that night, I've been obsessed with fire.

Not in the itching to burn things way, more in the 'I wound up being a firefighter' way. You'd think after nearly burning to death at twelve, I'd be mortally terrified of anything bright orange. I never even had nightmares about it. Some kids who escape house fires without even having a close call have nightmares of fire for years. How I went from hopelessly trapped behind a wall of flames to being blasé about it, even fascinated by fire, I don't think I'll ever understand.

Mom called it a miracle, as did most of her friends. I found out later that the trailer two spaces to the right of ours had an E-Meth lab in it, which exploded. Take methamphetamines and crank them up with magic, and you get E-meth, or 'enchanted meth.' Some people call it 'Cheth' or 'eldritch meth.' Whatever name you use, it's nasty shit. I hear it makes mages' spells go wild too, which is never good. Magic is unpredictable sober. High plus extra power? Bad, bad idea. When the drug factory went up, the trailers adjacent to it vanished entirely. The one right next to ours melted so fast, the old couple who lived in it never even knew what hit them.

Something bangs the wall next door with a loud *thud.* Tracy's ear-piercing verbal assault follows. What did she expect? Date an asshole, don't be all appalled when he acts like one.

So anyway, that's how I wound up working for the Philadelphia Fire Department. Big city, bigger fires. I've been at it ever since I graduated college. Couldn't decide what I wanted to do, so I have a generic 'liberal arts' degree. I didn't waste Mom's money though; I worked a night job stripping. No contact or anything, but $1,600 a week for waving my boobs around on stage for a couple hours a night was a no-brainer. Apparently, guys like my 'look.' I've always thought of myself as average. I'm not that tall, nor am I short. Not too thin, not too fat. I had a guy describe me as 'sinewy' once. Another guy called me 'lithe.' As far as I'm concerned, the only striking feature I have is my paleness. Everyone always assumes I have whiteface on. Sigh.

Oh, and my eyes are a little big. Gets everyone thinking I'm still seventeen. That is *extremely* annoying. I can't hate them too much though. They are two big reasons why the cops let me slide so much as a kid. I can do the 'innocent' look quite well.

It took me two years being officially part of the Philadelphia Fire Department before I did anything more than clean trucks or answer phones. Despite my times and scores on the training range being in the top five, I got coddled. The old lieutenant in charge of my stationhouse, Pirelli, didn't want 'the kid' to get hurt, or have a dead female firefighter on his hands. I almost got fired when I snuck onto the back end of Ladder 13 on a four-alarmer in the warehouse district. No one noticed I'd participated in the containment effort until after we got back. Lieutenant Pirelli reamed me out. Verbally.

The guys stood up for me though, said I pulled my weight. (If you ask me, I pulled well more than my weight.) But that's all behind me now. Pirelli jumped at a chance to make Captain out in the sticks somewhere west. Our new lieutenant, Andrew Sims, has no such hang-ups about sending me in.

So, I'm accepted (more or less) at my job.

I'm happy (more or less) being alone.

Why do I still feel uneasy? It's annoying, and it's been that way as long as I can remember. The little bastard in my head is why I got into so much trouble. Noise in my brain or something. I simply can't sit still doing nothing. If I do, that weird feeling comes back. It's like when you go to work but can't remember if you left the coffee machine on, and wonder if you're going to get home to a pile of smoking ash. Or, as Mom would say, it's like emailing her latest manuscript off to the publisher and finding a typo two seconds after she clicks send. It also kind of feels like a cop following me for six miles, wondering if he knows what I did three intersections ago or saw that thing I did with the beggar.

Oh, not like homeless beggar. I mean those annoying people who put on the bright orange vests and stand in traffic at stoplights trying to prey on a captive audience. It's hilarious to give their buckets a telekinetic whack and throw money everywhere. Let 'em scramble around trying to pick shit up with cars driving over it all.

Okay, so perhaps I do have a bit of road rage. Did I mention I've been known to have a short temper sometimes? Except with Mom. I can never bring myself to be pissy with her. Something about her presence is like balm on a rash. Even though I'm twenty-three, she can still hold me and I stop worrying about everything. That constant irritating unease? Yeah, it goes away when I'm with her. Sometimes it's tempting to move in back home—even if she did buy a house way off in Allentown. Living with my mom would help ease my mind, and especially in this economy, not having to pay rent would rule. But, I don't wanna be that kid that never moves out. Plus, as long as I keep my mind occupied, it's fine.

Relatively fine. Truthfully, it sucks, always feeling like I forgot something important or something *really* bad is going to happen to me any second.

The shouting next door alternates from Tracy to Asshole for a few minutes. Something else crashes into the wall, followed by a barrage of Tracy's shouting. I curl my feet over the side of the coffee table, daydreaming about storming in there and telling them both off. How can I pay attention to a show I've seen a hundred times already with all that noise?

A child's tearful wailing yell undercuts the shouting. Damn. Now I feel guilty. That poor kid. She can't be older than nine. I've only caught glimpses of her here and there, and don't remember any bruises, but hearing her cry-scream at her mother to 'please stop fighting' is getting under my skin. She has the same skinny threadbare look I use to rock at her age. Not a lot of money; not a lot of food.

Not my kid.

Not my problem.

Or it shouldn't be. The longer I sit here hearing that little girl cry, the more likely I am to do something stupid.

I have to get away from that madhouse.

Time to go for a walk.

2

SCARY

In a hurry to get away from the screaming, I grab a hoodie, step into my flip-flops, and head out the door. The majority of my non-work wardrobe consists of short skirts and some manner of leg-covering from fishnets to yoga pants, plus either Doc Martens, combat boots, or flip-flops. At the moment, I lack the patience to change, so the world will have to suffer me in sweat pants.

Killing that perv years ago didn't bother me. Maybe because I have no idea how I did it or even really *if*. I'd like to think I did it and he didn't simply suffer a coincidental massive cranial aneurysm as soon as I wanted the piece of shit to die. Hey, it could happen. Dead people in fires don't bother me at all, unless they're kids… but thank whatever powers that be I haven't had to witness that yet. Even lamb annoys me. Like, at least let the damn sheep grow up first before you kill it for food, right?

It has to be Mom's doing. She's so nurturing. If I got anything from her, it's that need to protect the weak or innocent. Once you're an adult, sorry pal, not my problem. I mean, as a professional firefighter, hauling citizens out of burning buildings *is* my problem. Irritating neighbors, not so much. I'd never yawn and leave some poor idiot to burn to death. More like if shit happened beyond my control, I wouldn't like be a wreck over it.

I head out my door into a narrow hallway that smells like a mixture of spaghetti sauce and beer farts. Tracy screaming, Asshole screaming, and her daughter begging them both to stop are still noticeable, though not as overbearing. A particularly loud wail of 'please don't hit her' from the kid gets me to clench my fists and stuff them in my sweatshirt pockets. Head down, I force myself to trudge to the stairs and jog the six flights to the ground floor.

Cold wind meets me outside, fluttering my hair to the side. It's early March, and Old Man Winter hasn't quite gotten around to screwing off for the year yet. Brr. Bare midriff and flip-flops aren't made for this kind of weather. A couple of tenants from the next apartment tower hang around the front porch across the street. One of them's got shorts on. Ugh, how can he stand that?

I get the usual 'hey babys' and whistles as I go by. Half of me wants to get pissed at them for the objectification, but the rest of me adores being thought of as pretty. Though, I doubt they mean it as a sincere compliment. They'd catcall just about anything with boobs. The indignant half pushes up to an indignant two-thirds, and I give them a sour look on my way by.

With nowhere specific in mind to go other than out of earshot of the war raging in apartment sixty-five, I wind up hiking all the way to the end of the block, crossing the narrow alley that cuts it in half. Yeah, apartment sixty-five is next to me. I'm in number sixty-six. On the sixth floor. I thought it was cool. Mom doesn't like it though. She can be superstitious, especially about things like that. I never understood it really. Whenever someone goes off on the religion thing around me, I tend to roll my eyes and walk the other way. But hey, it makes Mom happy.

An overbearing glow from inside Kwan's Market bathes the corner in near-daylight, almost painful to look at amid the sea of darkness in this part of town. Channeling my inner moth, I'm drawn to the light and decide to go inside.

The owner, a middle-aged guy, looks up from his Scry, an

enchanted slab of glass most of us use to read novels, play little games, or talk to people far away. Mind you, some do go for the electronic versions. They are a quarter the price, but the batteries run out. A Scry needs a new power gem once every three years.

His green Philadelphia Eagles shirt looks like someone hit his condiment counter with a Mayhem Jinx when he'd been standing too close. He smiles at me, and I return it. Every time we make eye contact, I calm down a little. I don't really know the guy too well, but I have a strong feeling he's nice, honest, and wouldn't hurt a fly.

I also think he's worried about his elderly parents.

Oh, I'm pretty sure I can read minds, too. Or not so much *read* as understand who I'm looking at, like how I knew in an instant that the perv wanted to hurt me. In retrospect, maybe I shouldn't be so jealous of anyone with magical gifts. Sure, what I can do isn't flashy—it's not even visible—but it can come in damn handy. If our trailer hadn't burned down, I would've made a hell of a detective. But, yeah... I don't have a wonderful relationship with laws.

Spray painting penises all over the police chief's car when I was fifteen kinda pissed him off. He remembered me two years ago and bitched when I got on the fire department. Tried to get me fired, but since I'd been a minor at the time, he had nothing solid. I guess 'oh pay no attention, you know kids do stupid things' only counts for boys.

Mr. Kwan buries his face in his Scry again. A glimmer of eldritch light dances around the edge of the device, tinting the whole area around him yellow. I wander the shelves, my hands still in my hoodie pockets. Having come here with nothing specific in mind, I scan for anything that catches my eye. Hopefully, by the time I'm head-bangingly bored with casing a convenience store at almost 10:30 p.m. under the oversaturated glare of three times the amount of life-sucking fluorescent lights a place this size needs, my neighbors will have yelled themselves quiet.

Hearing that kid next door plead has notched my mood up into a bad place. I have my darker moments, and I have daydreamed (probably too often) about doing cruel, unseemly things to random halfwits. It does scare me somewhat how close to 'hey, I could do this,' it feels sometimes. Like all that stands between me and sticking something long, narrow, and pointy into people like that judgy bitch from 52nd street is a shrug and a 'meh, fuck it.' Being called a hooker because my midriff is showing got under my skin.

So far, every time I've come close to doing something bad, I think of Mom and how disappointed she'd be in me. It's worked so far. Maybe I'm a sociopath? Maybe I should be on meds? Nah. Socios have no emotion, and I get plenty pissed off—or like in the case of the kid next door—guilty. Tracy's lying in a grave of her own digging, but her daughter doesn't deserve it.

Argh!

I swipe a canister of quick oatmeal off a shelf and get millimeters from hurling it across the room before I catch myself. Easy, Brooklyn. Easy. I let a lungful of air out my nostrils and set the almost-projectile down.

Doughnut. Yeah. That sounds good. I'll nab a doughnut and coffee. I need to drink almost an entire pot to notice caffeine anyway, so one small cup to wash down an empty calorie bomb won't keep me up too late. Not like I won't be awake 'til at least 1 a.m. anyway. Can't help it. Being a night owl sucks when my shift starts at seven.

At the back end of the store, Kwan's got a two-pot brewer right next to a case of doughnuts that have probably been sitting since earlier this morning, or at least this afternoon. I poke around until I locate a Boston cream that isn't too stale. After dropping it in a little wax paper bag, I pour myself a coffee—black of course—and put a cap on it.

Chimes announce the door opening. Two guys stride in, heading over to the register. I can't see much more than a wool hat and a black hood over the tops of the shelves from here. I collect my treat and coffee, and proceed to the register between an aisle packed with pet food on the left, and paper goods on the right. The end-caps have beef jerky, cat food, and snack cakes. Wow, organizational fail much?

Wool Hat guy moves to stand a bit to the right of the register and whips out a large silver handgun, before trying to pick Kwan's nose with it. The other guy hovers near the case of lottery scratch-off cards on the left, holding an empty plastic bag, as if expecting Mr. Kwan to fill it.

Both guys look somewhere between eighteen and twenty, one white, with the gun, one Hispanic. I get a sense of fear from them, and the intention to steal. Oh, yay for psychic abilities.

The armed one wags the pistol at the shopkeeper, yelling, "Come on, man. Hurry the fuck up!"

I walk over to the register into the nice convenient open spot the thugs left between them. After setting my food on the counter, I hold my keyring out, dangling my AATM crystal on its little keychain holder. "Hey, Kwan. Just a donut and a small coffee."

My indifferent smirk must have caught the guys off guard, as they stop being all fidgety, and stare at me. Mr. Kwan blinks, once, twice, his face almost as pale as mine. Aww. He's worried about me. That's so sweet.

"You got some balls, bitch," says the white guy. When I don't react, he swings around, putting the gun in my face. "I said, you got some balls, bitch."

I glance out of the corner of my eye at the .45 barrel an inch or so away from my cheek. Oh, screw this guy. I'm already in a bad mood. My telekinesis wraps around his whole arm, and I make the weapon angle upward before forcing his elbow to bend back so the gun presses against his temple.

"Didn't your parents teach you not to wave those things in a girl's face?" I give him an exaggerated once-over. "My, that's a rather big gun. Are you trying to make up for something else being small? No shame, man!"

He trembles from the strain of fighting me for control of his arm. Don't bother, pal. I shoved a pickup truck out of a parking space once after the shithead cut Mom off. The man screams, his stare locked on his gun, but he can't pull it away. Howling, he grabs his right wrist with his left and tugs; I smirk, and keep the pistol right where I put it.

Mr. Kwan goes weak in the knees. The poor guy looks ready to faint.

Bang.

Pain stabs me in the back of the left shoulder. It hurts like a huge guy hauled off and punched me, but there's blood on the front of my sleeve. I catch a glimpse of the Hispanic dick's reflection in the lotto ticket case. A small black revolver in his hand wobbles like a Chihuahua on amphetamines, a wisp of smoke trailing up from the barrel.

The son of a bitch shot me.

Oh, *now* I'm pissed.

"You're about to have a bad day," I snarl in Spanish.

A tiny tweak of telekinesis nudges the trigger on the .45, and Moron One's brains leap over the ceiling, floor, and a shelf of toilet paper. His buddy shrieks in terror and tries to shoot me again, but his bullet goes high, shattering glass somewhere behind me. In an instant of total rage, I grab him bodily with my telekinesis and pour all my fury into *away.*

The man sails out the door, spinning head over sneakers. Unfortunately, he doesn't make it to the other side of the street due to an unexpected meeting with a passing PEPTA bus. The *whump* of him getting intimate with the windshield makes me feign a cringe.

I look at Mr. Kwan and again hold out my AATM crystal. "Sorry about that."

Numb, he stands there, staring at me.

"Okay then." I lean over the counter and ring myself up while the shopkeeper continues doing a perfect impression of a statue. "I walked a whole block for this coffee and doughnut; I'd rather not leave empty-handed."

Once the AATM reader gem glows purple, I hold my crystal in the cloud of shimmering blue light it projects upward. The magic confirms my aura, the computer chirps, and my bank account gets lighter by $4.38.

"Thanks, Mr. Kwan. You might want to call the police." I wave at him, smile, and walk out. "Guy must've been on e-meth to shoot himself in the head like that."

I kinda feel sorry for him. Death freaks most people out.

Maybe it should freak me out too. Is it bad that it doesn't?

How warped is it that I'm ready to twist someone's head off because the asshole next door made that kid cry, but watching Moron One's head pop like a ketchup packet under a car tire is borderline funny? Okay, it wasn't so much the explosion of goop, but the look on the guy's face.

Yeah, I guess I am a little messed up in the whole empathy department.

Sigh.

Even in this part of Philadelphia, a gunshot will trigger Transpresence calls to the police. And I'd rather avoid the hassle— especially with a bullet in my arm. Well, a bullet *hole*. I'm pretty sure it came out and kept going into the wall. Speaking of which, I need to get home and clean that out. Maybe I ought to dig my DNA out of the wall, but that slug could be anywhere. By the time I found it, the cops would be swarming all over. Besides, I'm sure Kwan has cameras, plus he's seen me. Not to mention, as far as anyone knows, one guy offed himself and the other guy... well, that's a bit harder to explain, but he did shoot me first. Self-defense, right? Maybe it would wind up working out for me if they did dig that slug out of the wall with my blood on it. If anyone comes trying to bust my ass, I'll be like 'no, *I'm* the victim.'

Speaking of. I've never been shot before, and it surprises me how little it hurts. Nothing like the sheer agony they show in the movies.

I hurry down the block, managing to evade the notice of the small crowd that's formed around the PEPTA bus. The Philadelphia Enchanted Public Transportation Authority's safety stats for the year are going to take a hit. Oops. Suppose I'm doing okay. It's been thirteen years since I'd killed anyone. On the upside, I didn't really miss it, and I didn't get any sort of thrill out of it this time. In fact, dragging my trash out to the curb gives me a stronger feeling of having accomplished something. And I hadn't intended on Moron Two finding a bus. I guess that's karma in action.

Yeah, okay, they were human beings too, and they might still have parents, friends, or relatives who care about them, but they should've thought of that before they shot me. I have a mother and one friend who care about me too. So, poo. And hey, maybe the guy lived. The bus wasn't going *that* fast.

I give nothing in particular a raspberry as I scurry across the alley. Damn. I really hope the neighbors have settled down. If not, I will need to rely on the calming powers of sugar and coffee. A short woman with dark brown skin and a frizzy explosion of hair coming the other way gives my bleeding arm a long stare, but doesn't risk saying anything. I guess I finally look adult enough. Then again, they did that experiment three blocks away from here a few months ago where they set a little girl loose dressed up like a lost child and filmed people's reactions. Everyone ignored her, even when she tried approaching strangers to ask for help.

What the hell is wrong with this city?

I've got myself fuming again by the time I reach my building, but six flights of stairs saps my anger back to mere annoyance. I boot the door at the top, and it swings out of my way with its usual squeak. The stairs connect to the middle of a corridor around a corner from mine. I head to the right and round a ninety-degree left.

The kid from next door is out in the hall. She's wearing a cartoon-print oversized t-shirt for a nightgown, and sitting on the floor with her back against the wall opposite her apartment, swishing her bare feet side to side. Straight brown hair covers the characters on her chest, almost reaching the floor. She swivels her head toward me and looks up, staring.

I can tell she's frightened. The intention wafting off her is to not get hurt. She's out here because she feels safer, less afraid of some random stranger walking by than being in her own home.

Grr.

A scowl forms on my face as I trudge over.

The closer I get, the more the girl's fear shifts origin: me. Another feeling rises in her head. She wants help.

This is so not my problem. I just killed two men, well, definitely one. *Maybe* two. My night doesn't need to get any more complicated. After giving the girl a pleasant 'hello' smile, I sidle up to my door and try to hold the donut bag and coffee in my left while shaking my keyring around one-handed with my right.

"You're scary, but not bad scary," says a small voice right behind me.

I almost drop my honestly-gotten loot. Wow, it *still* feels weird to actually pay for things. It's amazing how easy it is to get away with shoplifting as a telekinetic. Collecting myself, I spin on the little kid who'd snuck up on me. "What?"

She fidgets at her t-shirt, pulling it tight around her legs, letting go, doing it again. "You're kinda... you know, scary, but I'm not as scared of you as I'm scared of Frank."

That must be Asshole. "Why are you out here in the hallway? It's almost eleven. You should be in bed."

"Frank's gonna hurt me," says the child to her feet. "He always looks at me bad. You're scary but nice." She peers up at me with a cowed posture, as if she expects me to take a swing at her. "I'm Ashley."

I sigh, and squat down to eye level. Maybe that'll make her less frightened of me. "Hi Ashley. I'm Brooklyn. If that man is hurting you, you should Teep the Police."

"I'll get in trouble. I'm not allowed to use the Transpresence machine." Ashley bites her lip and stares once more at the rug. "He hasn't like hurt me yet, but I *hate* the way he looks at me." She shivers.

We stand in silence for a few seconds. The guy probably resents having a kid around when he's trying to get Tracy naked.

The child lifts her gaze to me again, a nervous smile on her face. "You wouldn't be scared of Frank."

"No, probably not."

She stares at me with an odd intensity, almost awe. "What will you—?"

"Ash?" The kid's bottle-blonde mama sticks her head out the door of apartment sixty-five. At least she's managed to avoid a facial bruise this time, though she didn't quite get all the dried blood out of her nostril. "What are you doing out there? You scared me to death! Come on, get in here."

"Bye," whispers Ashley, waving to me.

"Sorry about that. I hope she wasn't bothering you," says Tracy.

"No. She wasn't. What's bothering me is how in need of a decent meal she looks." I stand from my squat and fix my dear neighbor with a stare. Her thoughts swim with worry and shame. The look on my face must be hot enough to melt steel, because she ducks out of sight as soon as she tugs Ashley inside.

Why was that kid staring at me like that? Oh, probably mystified by the bullet wound in my arm. And dammit. My coffee's getting tepid. I duck inside my unit, lock the door, and kick my flops into the corner. After padding into the kitchen, I enjoy my self-treat while there's still some heat left in the brew. Screw it. This apartment came with a rune oven. A minute on purple, and the java will be steaming again.

I stick the coffee in the little oven above my stove and tap the violet crystal on the console before hurrying to the bathroom. They say the kind of magic those things throw off will cause phosphorescent skin mold if you stand too close to them, but I don't believe the conspiracy nuts.

In the bathroom, I fish a box of adhesive bandages and some alcohol out of the medicine cabinet. How much can it hurt to clean out a bullet wound? Oh, drat. The stick-on bandages are probably not going to be enough for this. Sigh. I'm going to be pissed if I need to go to the hospital. They get so invasive about gunshot wounds. After removing my sweatshirt and dropping it on the floor, I lean my arm up to the mirror… and blink.

Blood smears in trails down to my wrist, but I can't find a hole. A twist gives me a look at my tricep, where the shot hit me, but there's no wound there either, merely more smeared blood.

Whoa. This is too tweaked.

Oooh, wait. I bet, Mr. Kwan's a Lifemage, and what I assumed to be stunned staring had been meditation. Yeah. That has to be it. I protected him so he healed me. Great. What the heck is a Lifemage doing managing a convenience store? Well. Enough with that.

I have a date with a doughnut.

3

INFERNO

The call came in at 1:07 p.m. the next afternoon.

A fifty-two-story hotel built almost a century ago decided to go all Roman candle. Is it bad of me to welcome the escape from a crew of guys telling me for an umpteenth time how striking my dark sapphire eyes are against my paper-white mug? Or that I'm too delicate and pretty to be a firefighter? At least the catcalls stopped a year ago after I threw Lamar out of his chair while arm wrestling.

By 1:12 p.m., I'm suited up in full regalia and humping it up the stairs behind my fire-buddy Jason Dunn. He's been with the brigade seven years now, signed on soon after turning eighteen. His stationhouse is across town from mine, but we run into each other often enough. I suppose that's a bad thing since us meeting technically means someone's shit is burning to the ground.

There's still a bit of 'protect the girl' going on, as the lieutenant has sent us to the twenty-ninth floor to do room checks and make sure none of the guests are sticking around. The flames are chowing down on hotel between the thirty-first and thirty-eighth, advancing toward the roof. Fire tends to burn upward much faster than it goes down.

Being under the burn leaves the stairwell relatively clear, though the stink of burning plastic and wood is strong. A handful of civilians scramble down past the line of yellow-coated firefighters. Pair by pair, we break off and enter floors. Most of these guys are from other station houses; this burn's pulled in every engine within eighteen miles, plus a few Hydromancers providing helicopter support.

A surprising percentage of victims tends to ignore alarms. I'm not sure if it's excessive fire drills at work that get them thinking of the flashing lights and bleeping as an irritation instead of 'get the hell out so you don't die.' Maybe humanity has simply reached the point where large numbers of people really would rather snuff it in a burning building instead of miss five minutes of reality TV—or whatever else someone inside a hotel room at one in the afternoon would be doing.

Word comes over the radio in my helmet that a group is trapped on the fortieth floor, close to the top of the fire, like sausages in a frying pan. Three lieutenants and a handful of chiefs direct firefighters by name, arranging a coordinated attack to push the fire away from a possible rescue point. They've got three Hydromancers on site now, all of them redirected to hammer the floor directly under the endangered civilians in an effort to buy time.

Since our names aren't mentioned, Dunn and I continue heading for our assignment at the twenty-ninth. I hate being coddled. Of all the responders on scene, I've got to be the least nervous in here. Almost all of them are terrified inside. Any human being would be. It's natural. What sets us apart from the average citizen is we're willing (and able) to set that terror aside and charge *into* an inferno to get as many survivors out alive as possible.

Only, for me, it's different. I'm not the least bit scared. I'm more scared of not being scared, if that makes any sense. Being in a burning building gives me the eerie comfort that I'm exactly where I am supposed to be. That whole permanent sense of unease I mentioned before? Yeah, it's gone inside a fifty-two-story inferno. Then again, I only get that gnawing irritation in silent calm, and those two words don't exist in a place like this. Nothing about a burning hotel is silent or calm. Between the constant bleep-buzz of the alarm, the distant roar of the conflagration a few floors up, the thunder of helicopters, and random breaking sounds, it's a chaotic mess.

The radio's an unintelligible chorus of firefighters and bosses trying to shout over each other. Dunn and I have a buddy channel. If we talk on it, it'll auto-mute the general broadcast so we can hear each other. Critical for life-and-death reactions, especially when two lieutenants are angling for captain next year and trying to be Commander General Hero over the open channel.

For the most part, idiots like that tend to get ignored. We do what we need to do when we need to do it, and if Lieutenant Big Head gets too far out of line, there's usually a captain around to knock them down a peg.

Jason ducks through the door at our floor. The air inside is hazy. He hesitates a second. Hmm. The fire's picking up speed.

"Uh oh. Guess it's not as clear as they thought," he says on our channel before switching to the broadcast and yelling, "We got smoke on twenty-nine. Heads up on Thirty."

"Roger," says another man.

"I got left," I say.

We advance down the corridor, booting open doors one by one. The hotel's system has released all the magnetic locks with the fire alarm activated, but every so often, there's a malfunction or an idiot tenant who's tripped the deadbolt. My third door has such an idiot.

A good, solid punt bashes the door in.

"Holy shit," mutters Dunn.

"What?" I send over the radio before yelling, "Fire Department, get your ass out of here, now!"

Bed's unmade, wisps of black smoke puff out of gaps in the drop ceiling. Shit, the fire has to be on the thirtieth by now. I can feel it chewing right overhead. We don't have a lot of time before this floor becomes a broiler.

"Fire's moving down," I say over the radio. "Black smoke seeping out of the ceiling on the twenty-ninth."

"Copy that. Yeah, we see it," says the same man who'd 'rogered'

Dunn before. "Fireball moving up the hallway. We're not going to be able to get to the east side."

"Come on, Amari, move your ass," yells Dunn.

I spin to check the bathroom. Naked fat guy lying in bloody water, wrists slashed. "Got a body here," I say over our private channel. "He's already checked out." While hoofing it to the next door on the left, I add, "Suicide, not fire."

"Poor fuck." Jason's five rooms ahead of me since none of his doors wound up bolted.

Yeah. This poor guy's first day as a ghost, and the place he chose to haunt is probably going to be torn down. While wondering what becomes of ghosts when their buildings are demolished, I make short work of a few doors before a heavy *thud* comes from the hallway outside.

"You okay?" I yell, rushing out of another empty room.

Jason punts a door again. "Bolted." He pounds on it, yelling, "Fire department. You have to get out!" He kicks it a third time, but the door holds.

"Move!" I run into a stepping side-kick that almost takes the door completely off its hinges. It flies open and embeds in the wall.

"Mother of fuck." Dunn stares at me. "How did you do that?"

"Uhh, Taekwondo classes?"

Before I can steal his room, a woman's scream comes from a good way down the hall.

"Shit," I say. "I got it."

I sprint toward the shouting woman, sailing past a four-way intersection and an elevator area. Copious billows of inky smoke swell out from the seams in the metal doors. Shit twice. That's not good. We've got minutes before this floor's glowing.

"This is Drake. The thirtieth is gone. Fire everywhere. Twenty-nine, stay alert. It's about to get warm down there."

"Copy," I say over the radio.

The screaming leads me to a door on the left three-quarters of the way down the length of the post-elevator hallway. Heavy, sooty smoke seeps between gaps in the drop ceiling tiles. The door opens with ease, and I barge in on a bone-thin woman tied down to the bed with bright red nylon straps. She's topless, and it's hot. Not *that* kind of hot. The kind of hot where her edible panties have melted and patches of wall are blackening.

A man lays face down beside the bed with a syringe still sticking out of his arm. Drug paraphernalia is all over the table between the two beds. As soon as I look at Mr. Needle, I can tell he's dead. Zero whispering of any sense of thought in that head.

She screams, thrashing at the restraints. "Help!"

Yeah no shit, lady, why do you think I'm here? "Stay calm. You're gonna be okay."

I rush over and grab the sex-shop tie-down. Tiny padlocks secure wrist cuffs, but a good yank rips them away from the part that goes around the mattress. Geez, cheap. As panicky as the woman is, I'm shocked she didn't get loose already. Then again, she's maybe eighty pounds. Meth's a shitty way to meet your maker. If you're gonna buy a ticket to hell, don't go coach. I rip the chintzy restraints off and scoop her up. She's probably a user as well, prominent ribs, looks thirty going on fifty, and I barely register the weight of carrying her.

"Luis!" she shouts.

"Sorry, ma'am. Luis is already gone." I pivot to carry her feet-first out the door, and haul ass to the stairwell access at the end. "Dunn, where you at?"

"Be there in a minute, checkin' all the left side rooms you slacked off on." His voice conveys a grin, so I don't bite his head off.

"Got a live one here. We need to get her out." I set the woman on her feet.

She streaks down the stairs as soon as I let go. Shit, lady. I don't know what's down there… I'm about to yell at her to wait, when a tremendous *crash* comes from behind me, shaking the floor. It feels like the entire hotel sways from the impact. I raise an arm to shield my facemask from a brilliant orange flash.

"Ugh," says Dunn over the radio. "Fuck. I'm hit."

"Jason!" I shout.

A second or two later, the flare fades, revealing a good portion of ceiling has caved in. Huge blocks of concrete slab decorate the hallway, and fire glows from most of the open doorways. The world above me has become a scene straight out of *Dante's Inferno*. Luminous clouds of fire shimmer from bright to dark orange, swimming around each other like living creatures. I stall in my tracks, mesmerized by the danger, the beauty. Only the rasp of breath in my mask reaches my ears; the rest of the world has become silent.

The blaze looks at me, recognizes me.

I feel like I've seen a wall of fire once like this before. Once when I'd been a little girl, but the memory is fleeting.

"Amari!" yells Dunn. "Get out of here before it all comes down! I'm pinned."

Squinting into the glare and smoke ahead, I spot Dunn half-buried under a pile of former ceiling. An I-beam lays across slabs of concrete, pipes, and wires. He's trapped up to the thighs.

Deep crackling emanates from random places above me in a rapid staccato; I picture concrete breaking apart. The floor at my feet vibrates with heavy grinding. The twenty-ninth is losing structural integrity. Any second now, we're going to be on the twenty-eighth. Buildings like this can pancake if it gets hot enough. One floor gives out totally, and it'll take everything below it down to the ground.

Dunn does *not* have time for me to get backup.

"This is Captain Walters. Everyone out!" comes over the radio. "That's an order."

Jason lifts his head at the death rattle of the building. He knows it too. "Get out of here, Amari. I'm fucked."

"No you're not!" I sprint for him.

A large blur falls toward me, knocking me into a stagger, but I keep my balance, swatting it aside with an *oof*. When I'm about ten feet from the debris pile, a room door pops open in a blast of fire. I cringe away from it, but it wraps around me. Not too bad, only a little toasty. No pain.

I power past it and skid to a halt by the mountain of debris. Dunn's eyes are huge white spots in the grime covering his clear facemask.

"Get the fuck out of here, Amari! This is my last ride, babe." He waves both hands in a repetitive 'go away' gesture.

"No." I stare at the I-beam and lock onto it with my telekinesis. If I can shove a truck out of a parking spot, I can move this.

He screams as the beam shifts. Concrete dust pulverizes around it, but it jerks only a few inches back and forth. I gasp, grunting like I'm trying to lift a 400-pound barbell without special powers. Dammit, it's wedged. He shouts again, pain mixed with panic.

The floor shudders like an earthquake.

Damn it. "I'm not leaving you here. You're not dead yet!"

For all the good it'll do, I lurch forward and grab the I-beam with my bare hands. I have to move this thing. I have to pull it away so he can survive.

I.

Will.

Not.

Let.

Him.

Die.

My temples throb with a bizarre sensation. The first thought that filters past the 'must lift this' mantra is I've strained so hard I've given myself an aneurysm. A sharp yank rips the air hose away from the bottom of my facemask, pulling it down and twisting it so I can't see shit. The harness holding my air tank, and my firefighter's coat are torn off me to the rear. A hunk of concrete must've fallen on me.

"What the fuck!" shouts Dunn.

The I-beam gives way, rising. I'm lifting it. Telekinesis plus my arms. Holy crap. I'm doing it. I grunt, strain, pull, and...

Feel the metal bend between my fingers?

I blink.

What?

The I-beam comes clear of the mound of crap and I haul it into the air. It's much lighter without concrete on top of it. I pivot to the side and give it a toss before reaching up to fix my facemask. It refuses to sit properly; when I try to force it, my head twists. My frustration level goes from zero to 'break everything I can touch' in an instant. I rip the facemask off and hurl it to the floor. It falls through the hole the I-beam made, and tumbles to the twenty-eighth.

Holy shit. I lose two seconds staring at the damage the thing I just lifted caused. How heavy *was* it?

Dunn crawls backward from the debris pile, staring up at me like he's about to (or already has) loaded his pants.

"What?" I ask.

At that instant, it occurs to me that the ceiling is closer than it had been. I look down at myself. My hands have sprouted black talons, and the floor is farther away from my head than it ought to be. At a strange sensation of 'touch' I've never before realized, I shift my gaze to the left and catch sight of a wing, like a dragon's, mushed against the wall. A patch of sapphire light illuminates the spot, mirroring the motion of my head. I raise a hand to my face and it turns blue.

What on Earth? My eyes are glowing and I'm like seven feet tall now?

"Amari? Is that you?" breathes Dunn.

Another ripple of shuddering and crunching emanates from everywhere. The whole building is teaching itself how to breakdance.

"So they tell me." I'm not sure if he can hear me since my mask is one floor down. I'm about to take a step toward him when I get a sudden flash of insight that this entire hallway is a second and a half away from being full of fire. A strong gust of wind whips up out of nowhere and rips past me from the front.

My wings catch it and pull me back two steps.

With a thrust of my arm, I telekinetically shove Dunn. Hard. He zooms off down the corridor like a human torpedo. A tremendous roar builds behind me, and I barely have the time to whirl around and shield my face—with one arm and a wing—before the backdraft *explodes*.

I close my eyes, expecting this is the end of my line. But intense pain never comes. The sensation reminds me of a pleasant summer breeze. Small pieces of wood hit me and clatter away. Seconds later, when the push of wind dies down, I open my eyes.

Most of my clothes are smoking cinders. My boots kinda survived, but that's the extent of it. I'm more stunned by not feeling naked. Where bare skin ought to be, my chest resembles armored plates. I still have the general shape of breasts, but they're like made of snow-white Kevlar or something. Same with my arms and legs… and tail. Say what?

Tail!?

What the fuck am I?

Did I get a contact high from being in that druggie's room?

The floor lurches, about to drop out from under me.

Dunn's muted scream snaps my head around. He's scrambling to get a hold of something as the rug below him gives way, chunks of concrete falling. Above us, the heavy *thud, thud, thud* of pancaking floor slabs rumbles closer.

I'm not sure what makes me react, but I sprint straight at him. Oh, hell. I've got goddamned wings. I wonder if they work. He doesn't see me coming, which is probably a kindness. I'm more than a little freaked myself; I imagine seeing a whatever I am galloping straight at him wouldn't be a fun memory.

The floor starts to buckle under my steps the closer I get to him. Clawed toes grip the carpet, keeping me from sliding. When I reach him, instinct takes over and I hurl myself forward, dragging him. Somehow, I wind up flying horizontally down the remainder of the corridor, cradling Jason to my chest.

My left shoulder bears the brunt of our impact with the wall, and we smash clear through the cinder blocks to the outside amid a rain of small chunks. An instant after we're out, a blast of thick grey dust rushes out to surround us. Our floor just pancaked. Shit. I can't see a damn thing, but I can still feel gravity. With a lean, I trust my ears telling me there's open air in front, and dive. We clear the dust cloud in a few seconds.

Dunn lets out a scream far too high to have come from a man. We're twenty-nine stories in midair over the hotel courtyard. My wings stretch far to the sides, acting like a parachute. As if on autopilot, I steer into a spiral that bleeds off speed, heading for an open yard a short distance away on the other side of an empty street. Jason groans, keeps his eyes closed, and keeps muttering "holy shit" over and over. My desire to not smack into the ground slows us even further, as if reality or gravity listened to me. Wings flared, I extend my legs and glide into a landing in an alley half a block away from the fifty-two-story-high Roman candle. Somewhere out of sight in the smoke, the thudding of a helicopter continues.

Jason stops screaming a few seconds later. He uncurls himself from my embrace and stares into my eyes.

My reflection in his visor isn't as bad as I feared. By and large, my face looks the same, except my eyes are glowing pools of dark blue energy and I've got horns. They're maybe four inches with a slight curve, and onyx black like my claws and toe-talons. Hmm. Guess that explains my subconscious attraction to black nail polish.

"Amari?" he asks.

"Yeah." My voice sounds the same.

"Did that just happen?" He pulls his mask off and gulps down fresh air.

I look back at the inferno belching fire from windows wherever the building crumbles in fits and starts. The floors have collapsed to about the nineteenth, great plumes of dark grey dust and smoke shroud the structure like a cloak, creeping downward. By some miracle, the pancaking stopped before it went all the way to the ground. Shit, I hope they got those people out.

"If it didn't, we're having one weird-ass afterlife," I say.

"What are you?"

"Other than naked? I have no idea." I brush ash off my arm. Am I stuck like this? Or how can I change—

I shrink back to my normal five-foot-six. The armored chitin becomes skin, my wings go back to wherever they came from, and my tail feels like it retracted up into my spine. Now *that* is funky. The sensation leaves me squirming and paralyzed with 'ick.'

And quite normally naked.

Damn it's cold. Or… maybe it isn't. Maybe it's cold *to me.*

He drags himself upright, favoring his left leg. After shrugging off his air tank, he removes his long coat and offers it. "Here. You're, uhh, a little out of uniform."

"Uhh, thanks." I pull the coat on and close it. "Maybe we should keep this quiet huh? Like not tell anyone?"

Jason nods. "Sure, if you want. You saved my ass. Whatever you want me to say, I say."

4

TOO STRANGE

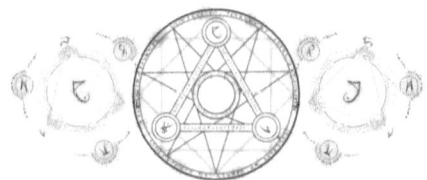

T he brass bought the excuse that something magical exploded in one of the rooms and wound up disintegrating most of my gear. It's true that cops tease their own when something goes wrong, but they got nothing on firefighters. I'll be hearing about the naked thing for the rest of my life, but hey, no one knows I'm a... whatever I am. Except Dunn, and I trust him.

I wound up dragging my highly-confused ass in the door of my apartment a little after nine at night, after we finished at the hotel. They managed to get most of the citizens out of that upper room, but lost seven. Six burned, one guy decided trying (and failing) to learn how to fly beat fire. Jury's still out on how it started, but in total, nineteen died. That's the best guess. Two old people had heart attacks, ten are missing-presumed-dead. I overheard some of the investigators discussing it while I'd been packing up to leave. They think the blaze started when something on the forty-second floor exploded.

The TV's been on for a while after I got back, whatever channel happened to be on last. A couple of guys in suits are talking about a 'case.' I haven't been paying enough attention to tell if it's a lawyer thing or a police drama. My brain hasn't stopped spinning around the bigger question:

What the hell am I?

Again and again, the sensation of standing there in the backdraft replays in my head. It's opened a Pandora's box of maybe-memories that I'm not sure I want to see again. When my childhood home burned, I'd been trapped in the back bedroom. If the thing had had wheels, my room would've been the rear end. The door out was three-fourths the length of the trailer away, part of the living room.

I stare straight through the television set and see the hallway from that place, that night. Shaggy brown carpet blackens in the flames before my eyes. The PlayStation controller dangles from my fingertips; a hot wind whips my hair back. For years, I'd pushed what had happened over the next few minutes out of my brain.

Guess I refused to believe it, too.

Standing there at the doorway of my bedroom, the only part of my home not yet engulfed in fire, I remember being terrified. I had nowhere to go—in front of me, everything burned. My room's only window had an air conditioner bolted into it from outside. I couldn't make a decision. Staying in my room equaled dead, but so did anything else. How many twelve-year-olds gaze at the moment of their imminent death and think, *Wow, that sucks?*

Something kept me from panicking, and after what happened this afternoon, it makes sense. A deep, inner part of myself must have known the fire couldn't hurt me. Why? Who bloody knows? The trailer had begun to collapse. The roof peeled apart on the right side and a cluster of flaming toilet-paper rolls bounced into the hallway out of the closet. One of them came to a halt on my bare foot, and it didn't hurt. That's what snapped me out of the haze.

I didn't have any pets, but I did have one precious thing: my PlayStation. After tossing it—and my controller—out the little bit of window between the frame and the AC, I ran down the hall. The fire torched my clothes when I got stuck under a collapsed pile of wall. By the time I dragged myself free, my pajamas were history. Now that I think about it, the jagged metal had been more of a threat to me than the burning.

Calm, and mesmerized by how pretty the fire was, I wandered

around the holes in the living room floor. I walked barefoot over glowing embers, and naked straight into active flames, right to a hole in the floor where the fire hadn't gone. On hands and knees, I crawled half the length of the trailer to a gap in the skirting, and made it outside, only a charred ring of fabric around my neck.

I remember thinking it looked stupid, so I broke it off and tossed it before anyone noticed me standing there. Running around with nothing on didn't bother me, still doesn't actually, at least not from an 'embarrassment' point of view. I generally don't because it's not considered 'cute' now that I'm grown up. Like I said, Mom had her hands full.

A crowd gathered by a row of police cars and fire trucks. Residents of nearby trailers. Mom had been there, sobbing hard on the shoulders of a cop who'd probably been holding her back from running inside after me. I'm sure the man had told her I'd died, since no one could've possibly survived a burn like that.

It must've been two minutes or so of me standing there shell-shocked, the bystanders and flashing lights melting into a blur of random color. Eventually, Mom noticed me. She screamed and pointed. At the sound of her voice, I took a few steps toward her before a fireman ran over and wrapped me up in an itchy blanket.

The rest of that night and the following day, I hadn't 'forgotten.' Mostly, it had been me saying "I dunno," a lot to a bunch of uniforms who wanted to know how I got out alive. At least blocking the memory out helped me lie. Was it technically lying since I couldn't make myself remember?

Bah. I really don't have the ability to think clearly right now.

Time swirls into a drain of nothingness as the probable truth of what happened that night orbits my head. I'm still having trouble opening the door and accepting it, but between the fire earlier today and me surviving back then, it has to be true. I already know I'm abnormal. Normal people can't move stuff with their mind or *know* what a person's intentions are by merely making eye contact with them.

Sudden inspiration launches me off the sofa. I run to the kitchen and turn one of the stove burners on. The metal coil goes from dark to glowing orange in a moment. Inch by inch, I ease my right hand closer, but it's more like I'm closing in on a fresh cup of coffee. My logical side screams at me to stop, but my arm keeps going. Mouth open, heart racing, I stand there feeling like I'm no longer in control of my body.

When my fingers touch the heating element, I start to scream—but it's purely mental. I'm not burning myself. No smoke, no melted skin. Whoa. The red-hot coil is like a hand warmer on a winter day or a cup of steaming tea. Still breathing in tiny, rapid sips of air, I lower the rest of my hand until it's covering the burner. Once I'm sure my skin isn't going to spontaneously combust, I shut off the burner and stare at the faint spiral smudge on my palm. Guess it's been a while since I cleaned the stove.

Oh, this is too freaky.

I guess I can't burn?

Okay. Experiment two.

Can I do that... other thing at will? Or only during 'oh shit' moments?

My air tank and coat made one thing clear. I need to give the extra parts room. To that end, I zip into my bedroom and grab a racer back top and a black lacy miniskirt. May as well go commando so the tail doesn't destroy a second set of panties in the same day. For the same reason, I skip shoes. Anything in here, *I* would have to pay to replace. My keys go into a hip pouch, and I'm out the door, heading for the roof.

Our stairwell that I loathe so much goes all the way up to the top of the building. There's supposed to be a padlock on the door, but someone broke it long before I moved in here and our super doesn't give a shit. I push the dingy brown door out of my way and stroll out under the night sky. Here, I'm fourteen stories above the ground and pretty well out of sight of everyone in the area, minus the birds, but they're awesome at keeping secrets. It's dark and uncomfortably chilly due to a continuous breeze. At least the air smells clean, free of trash, piss, or chemicals—an infrequent pleasure in this part of the city. The waist-high wall at the edge lets me force myself to peer over without panicking. Fire never scared me, but heights are another story.

I have wings. I might be able to fly. I'm scared of heights.

The complete ridiculousness of that hits me. My sudden, sharp laugh terrifies dozens of pigeons, which flee to the sky in a cloud of grey feathers. Some circle back and land, while most keep going off into the darkness.

Feet apart, arms out. Flex fingers. How does this work?

Eyes closed, I concentrate on wanting to have wings. A glimmer of energy inside my brain forms near the back of my skull. It feels about the size of a cherry tomato, sliding around and eluding me as I envision a mental 'hand' trying to grab it. Whenever I think I have it pinned down, it slips free. Over and over again, the gelatinous mass squidges out of my grip, almost as if it knows how I'm going to attack it before I do.

"Dammit!" I shout, my voice echoing a few times off the walls of nearby high-rises.

I lean against concrete, head bowed, hair fluttering in the wind as I stare down the length of my apartment building at the street. Maybe it has to be a 'stressful' situation? Would the wings work if I jumped?

No way am I trying that test. The burner's one thing; even if that had failed, a nasty burn to the hand could've been fixed by a Lifemage. Going *splat* on the sidewalk would be kinda final. Damn that thing in my brain.

Wait.

It's in my brain. Or it *is* my brain. No wonder it knows what I'm doing—it's me.

Again, I adopt a wide stance with my arms out a bit like a gunslinger. I want wings. The energy ball coalesces in the back of my thoughts. This time, instead of trying to 'grab' it, I try controlling the nugget of strange feeling directly. It slides down my spine, and a loud, *fwoof* breaks the silence.

A bit like I'd imagine opening a fourteen-foot-wide leather umbrella would sound like.

I don't have to open my eyes to know it worked. I've got two extra body parts complete with a sense of touch. The previously-mild wind has become an annoyance trying to push me over backward, but it's fairly easy to lean into it and keep my footing.

The thick leading edges of my wings are as pure white as the rest of my skin, though feel hard and smooth to my touch, like a crab shell. Dense black membrane spans between a few smaller interior spars, and a nine-inch curved talon sprouts from the main joint. When I stretch them out as far as I can, they reach more than my height in either direction. Folded, the talons at the bend are about three feet over my head, the tips an inch or two off the ground.

Well, damn. I stole the wings from a dragon.

A quick grab of my ass confirms the lack of a tail. A hand to my forehead confirms no horns there. I think about horns and feel that same odd tingle at my temples. Yep. Horns are there. When I want them 'away,' they disappear.

A wicked grin spreads across my face. Well, all right. This is kinda cool.

The racer-back shirt remains intact, since it exposes my shoulder blades on either side of a narrow strip of fabric. So, wings don't automatically mean tits out if I've got proper clothing. Good to know. Seeing these things with the presence of mind that comes with a lack of 'oh shit we're going to die!' is both amazing and unnerving.

A light scratch from my fingernails at the membrane almost hurts. It's sensitive, but thin. I bet it would heal even faster than a bullet in my shoulder. Speaking of which, I suppose the reason that healed is due to whatever the hell I am. Poor Kwan, guess he's not a Lifemage— which explains the convenience store. Prodding the membrane is about as comfortable as pinching the stretched web of skin between my thumb and index finger. Right. Protect the wing membrane. Damage there would be superficial, but painful.

Experiment three: normal me.

Putting the wings away comes far easier than finding them. A few seconds' worth of concentration causes them to collapse into a wing-shaped coalescence of black smoke, which rushes into my back. Neat.

I summon them again, this time keeping my eyes open, and discover the smoky thing happens when they appear. It's much easier the second time, and even easier the tenth. For a little while, I'm a four-year-old who found her mother's collapsible umbrella and went wild.

A metallic *squeak* echoes up from the edge. Probably one of our wonderfully-maintained balcony doors. I'm nosy, so I peer over the side, down at a bottle-blonde head at the sixth floor. As soon my attention focuses on her, the conversation she's having with a phone becomes clear to me.

"... know what to do. She's never pulled anything like that before," says Tracy, my neighbor.

Hmm.

I curl my fingers over the wall and crouch to make it harder to see me.

Tracy bobs her head while listening to the phone. "I caught her playing with candles."

A murmur emanates from her phone.

"Don't give me that 'all kids play with candles' crap. It's not a pyromaniac thing. She wasn't *just* playing with candles. My eight-year-old daughter had them set up on a pentagram! When I asked her what she was doing, you know what she said?"

She listens for a few seconds.

"Oh, that's funny." Tracy sighs. "She told me she was trying to summon a demon to make Frank go away."

Aww. That poor kid. That's so sad. I glance up at my wings. Hang on. The heck? Did that girl know something I didn't?

"Phase. Like hell!" yells Tracy. "Did any of *your* kids go through a devil-worshipping phase at that age? Fifteen, sixteen, sure... but *eight?*"

The voice on the phone gets loud enough for me to hear a woman snap, "*I* didn't shack up with a creep! You need to get Ashley away from that man."

"I don't need your judgment, Jo, I need advice!"

Oh, this is getting good. I lean up to listen better, but startle at the sense of 'hey, I'm not alone.' I gasp, whipping my head around to stare behind me, and my blood freezes in my veins.

In the shadows behind the small rooftop shed with the stairwell door, a tall, male figure stands in silhouette—except for glowing golden eyes. Who or whatever he is, I do *not* like the way he's staring at me. I can't ever remember being so damn scared of anything in my life.

For an instant, I'm a little kid about to be lured into a stranger's car again, only now I feel as terrified as I should have been.

The gold eyes narrow.

Shit!

Overcome by panic, I fling myself off the roof. Instinct takes over, stretching my wings. They catch my weight, letting me glide. Without the burden of a firefighter in my arms, I wind up flying instead of parachuting. It takes only a few seconds for the fright of that bizarre glowy-eyed stranger to wear off. I've got wings, and they work!

This is awesome!

Whoa, hang on, that building is coming up fast. Turn! Turn!

I flail my arms and shift my weight, but I have all the grace of a styrofoam toy glider some kid threw at a wall. An instant before impact, I manage to pull up, so I smack into the obstacle vertically. The meaty *slap* my crash makes resounds several times.

Somewhere above and behind me, a haughty-sounding man laughs. I'm in too much pain to move, and too frightened to dare try to open my eyes. The laughing fades into the distance; whoever he is, he's leaving me in peace.

That's weird.

Oh, and screw him for laughing at me.

A moment later, the stinging of the world's most severe belly flop fades. I risk peeking and find that my nails—hands *and* feet—have become claws, pierced into the bricks. I'm clinging to the twenty-somethingth story.

Okay, think. I'm flying better because I'm not carrying Jason, and my body isn't covered in bone armor. I can't steer because... I'm new at this? Wait, I remember something in biology class about birds. Hmm. Tail?

I concentrate on the idea of having my tail out. Initially, it feels like I'm about to drop a number two, but a bony edge scrapes at the back of my left ankle. I peer down, and sure enough, tail. It's a little disturbing, if I'm honest with myself. It's hairless, and the same white as the rest of my skin. Where it meets my spine, it's about as big around as my wrist, and it tapers to a little more than finger-width that goes into a shiny onyx barb that looks like the head of an ancient spear.

While adhered to the side of a building, I spend a few minutes getting the hang of working the tail. It's prehensile and quite flexible. It can stab like a knife, slash, coil around, and probably even grab things (though the bladed barb would get in the way). On a lark, I stab at the wall, and startle myself when the point goes four inches deep in the stone.

Holy shit. That thing is dangerous!

And… stuck.

I tug a few times, but it's not going anywhere.

Okay, if I *am* a demon, I'm like the world's worst demon.

That certainly does explain quite a few things. Blasé about killing, the fire thing, probably why I tried to have sex at fourteen. I say tried because Mom caught me, rather caught *us*. I brought Charlie Tavis from a couple trailers over to my bedroom. He'd come out of the blue with, 'hey, wanna do it?' I'd always been impulsive, and at the time, I was like, 'sure, why not. Sounds fun.' Mom walked in on us the exact instant he climbed up on top of me after we'd finished stripping. We'd both been staring at each other trying to figure out what went where.

She screamed, "Brooklyn Chloe Amari! What are you doing?" at me.

I didn't mean it to be flippant, in fact, I'd been dead serious when I looked at her, blinked, and asked, "What? are we doing it wrong? Am I supposed to be on top?"

Mom almost fainted. Probably because she knew I was serious. My not being embarrassed at getting caught made her embarrassment at being asked for advice ten times worse. So, yeah, Charlie never even talked to me again. Needless to say, we didn't do anything that night. Once Mom recovered, I got 'the talk.' I'll give the woman one thing. As much of a terror as I was, she knew the way to control me. Somewhere between telling me how much whatever I did hurt her and making me 'promise not to' do it again, I wound up listening. If she could get me to 'promise,' she won.

Anyway. Time to give this flying thing another go.

I chant, "You can fly. Don't be afraid of heights," to myself about ten times before springing away from the wall and stretching my wings.

My tail, which I'd forgotten remained stuck like King Arthur's sword, yanks me to an abrupt halt, and I slap face-first into the building for the second time. Only now I'm upside down and hanging by my tail.

Ow. This sucks.

I just about look up past myself at it when the blade slips free.

"Aaaaaah!"

The street rushes at my head. Every ounce of 'nope!' I can summon goes into my wings. The membranes cry out in agony, signaling like they're seconds from peeling away from the spars. I scream past clenched teeth and careen around in an arc that catapults me upward. Flapping doesn't seem to be doing much. My grace in the air feels like a pregnant milk cow on roller skates. Grunts and groans leak between my teeth as I fight for altitude. I'm getting some, but in small bits.

Eventually, I work out that *wanting* to fly upward does more than any amount of physical flapping or—yes, I admit it, I tried to 'swim.' The wings perform better at full extension without being flapped. Something magical is going on here. I think about a direction, and I go that way. The tail does help me steer, but maybe that's in my head. The onyx-bladed death noodle hanging out of my skirt seems more like a weapon than a flight-assist.

Seriously, I could take a dude's head off with that thing.

For kicks, I swipe at a fire escape with my tail as I go by. The bladed tip sparks on contact, but slices the steel railing. A minor jolt from the impact rides up my tail, but no worse than hitting a guy in the head with a baseball bat felt to my knuckles. Talk about a concealed-carry weapon.

Over the better part of the next hour, I acclimate to this newfound freedom. Collapsing my wings allows for fast dives, but for the most part, all I have to do is hold them out wide and 'magic' myself around. It's difficult to tell how fast I'm going, but I wouldn't be surprised if I were outpacing a car, at least in the city—but that isn't saying much.

Sometime in the future, assuming I don't wake up and find out this is all a dream, I'll need to time myself going between two points. I gotta know. Though, looming-big-dude with glowing gold eyes is my second WTF moment. Maybe I should get the hell out of the sky and lay low?

On that note, I pull around in a tight circle and race back to my building.

My bare feet clap on concrete as I land. Stings. All right, I came down a bit hard. I can improve on that. Hey, I went from flying face first into an apartment tower to pulling off some nifty aerial maneuvers in an hour. I'll get this worked out.

A seconds' concentration hides my wings and tail, and I once again look like a normal human.

Cool.

Only… I'm not a normal human.

I gaze up at the overcast sky, silent for a while, listening to the wind. My hair flaps over my face, but I ignore it. "What am I?"

Not that I expected an answer, but I don't get one.

Eventually, I bow my head. I can't decide if I should feel thrilled or worried. I take one more breath of crisp night air, and trudge back inside.

5

SECRET ADMIRER

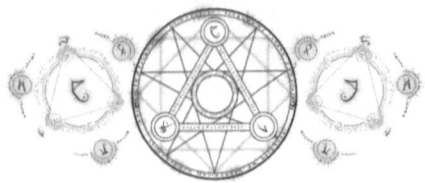

Thursday felt *too* normal. Other than an all-hands meeting to debrief everyone on the hotel blaze, my shift consisted of routine. Cleaning the stationhouse, checking hoses, making sure my replacement gear fit. They also sent me to Starbucks. Usually, a probie gets that detail, but being the only woman here, I somehow keep doing it. The only reason I put up with it is someone else pays for whatever I want, within reason, as long as I hoof it to pick up the order. But I *like* being bored at work. It means no one's life is in danger. All day, I keep looking over my shoulder for tall, dark, and golden-eyed.

Natalie, my best/only friend calls me Friday afternoon and suggests we go out. She's lucky on two fronts: she gets to set her own work hours, and if she screws up at her job, no one gets hurt. Usually. Okay, she's an enchanter, so I suppose if she *really* screws up, someone could theoretically get hurt—or turned into a fuzzy animal—but she's too careful for that. If anything, she'd keep the wild energies from going off in a random direction and blow her shop to bits before she let anyone else get injured.

Since I've had two days of relative peace—even the neighbors haven't been fighting—I say yes. I haven't seen Nat in a couple days, and she's tuned into my same broken wavelength. I'm more inclined to think it's been quiet next door more due to Frank not being around than the two of them trying to keep things calm for Ashley's sake.

My twelve-hour shift ends at six. Hey, it's not too bad. I have Monday off, and if there's nothing to do at the stationhouse, I'm officially allowed to sleep if I want. We even have a barracks upstairs. At least some part of my job is merely being there in case of an emergency. Sometimes, we fill the space with refresher training on stuff like CPR or working out in our pathetic little gym. Some of the guys also go for EMT certification.

I'd been tempted to skip taking the PEPTA bus to work Friday and fly, but broad daylight made me chicken out. A couple months ago, a cockatrice strayed into the city, and you'd have thought it heralded the end of the world. The giant green chicken of the apocalypse or something. Don't get me wrong, those things are nasty. Locking eyes with one can leave a person paralyzed for weeks. We had some courses on that. You wouldn't believe the number of Cockatrice Pulmonary Resuscitation jokes a guy can come up with in ten minutes.

What had really shocked everyone hadn't been the cockatrice in and of itself, but that a magical creature made it into the city. Back in ancient times, they roamed all over the place, but modern cities—at least the big ones like Philadelphia—have wards. Magical beasts can't get in. Like putting up an electric fence to keep cows in, or in this case *out*. Cops went nuts trying to find the breach, and they never did.

Of course, the mayor assured everyone all was well. The damn city could be burning all around him and that ass-kisser would try to tell everyone not to worry. What's truly sad is that about thirty percent of the Commerce party would happily agree with him. Too stupid to realize or too loyal to question. Sigh. I'm not officially a Populist either. I couldn't care less about politics; it's more watching stupid people act against their own self-interest that boggles my mind. One cockatrice walks down the street, and the Commerce side blames Mexicans while the Populists demand more money for infrastructure. Pity the Mage party is a laughingstock that'll never see office.

So, yeah, speaking of giant green ones... I chickened out of flying.

Rather than catch a PEPTA, I wait for Natalie's little cream-colored Scarab. A few minutes past six, she comes sliding around the corner two blocks away. She drives a little foreign car with a roundish shape that she enchanted to be even cuter. The headlights have eyelashes that blink, and I swear the thing's front bumper makes it look like it's smiling. She's also put in a ton of comfort enchantments.

I ooze in the passenger door and flop into a chintzy little bucket seat that feels like a high-end living room recliner. Two figurines, a princess and a unicorn, wander around her dashboard. Yeah. So, my best friend is girly as hell. She's a few months older than me—she turned twenty-four in February—but she usually dresses like she's twelve. Nat loves the frilled socks and white dresses.

Except when we go out. Tonight, she looks fairly normal: nice red dress that bares her left shoulder and short heels. I'm still rocking the fire department white polo shirt and black BDU pants.

"Hey." I unbutton my collar. "Need to hit the apartment and change."

"Really?" asks Natalie. "I thought you were going like that."

"Ha. Ha."

We stop at my place long enough for me to grab a black brocade blouse, matching choker, and a black lace miniskirt with black tights. When the two of us are hanging (and not going out), people never believe we're together. Girly-girl and the Doom Queen. That's her name for us anyway. Like I said, she's twenty-four going on twelve.

I examine my fingernails and make my claws pop out. Heh. Maybe I *am* the Doom Queen.

WE ARRIVE AT A NIGHTCLUB-SLASH-BAR NAMED NIFLHEIM AT TWENTY after seven. Natalie zips her little Scarab into the parking lot, and I swear what her hands do to the wheel does *not* correspond to where the car actually steers. She looks like a child with a pretend steering wheel half the time, which makes me think the car's running on mental command somehow, like my flying. Either way, we wind up in a parking space by this building that looks like someone tore it out of a thousand years ago.

The façade is stone, like a castle, with giant crossed axes mounted between each window. Heavy, white fog pours from the roof between the crenelations, falling in shafts down the side of the building to gather in a layer at the ground. Pulses of violet, red, and blue light flicker in the windows, brighter on the right side of the building.

"Wow. Where'd you find this slice of Heaven?" I ask. Whenever we go out, which these days is about twice a month, we take turns picking a place we've never been to before. "Looks gothic."

"Figured you'd like it." Natalie winks at me before patting the dashboard and whispering, "Okay, sweetie. Time for a nap."

The car shuts down.

When we get out, the distinct lack of skull-pounding music makes me smile. I *can* hear music, but only enough to know it exists inside, not pick out what the song is. That's a definite plus. Any place where it's so loud you can dance in the parking lot and feel like you're in the club is not for me. I guess I'm 'old' now. A couple years ago, ear-bleeding volume didn't bother me. Every bar and nightclub back home where I grew up in Quakertown knew me on sight. Back then, I didn't have real friends, just a group of high school outcasts who I did stupid shit with. Once they realized I had weak impulse control and no shame, the dares started.

So yeah, we got kicked out of a lot of venues.

Natalie takes point and zips across the parking lot to the end of the line waiting to get in. I don't know how on Earth she can move so fast in six-inch stilettos. The boots I matched to this outfit have like a three-inch (if that) heel, and I'm a little wobbly. Never did the girly thing. I should've stuck with the Doc Martens; they'd have fit this outfit, too. My fault for trying to dress up.

Bleh.

Eventually, we get to the door, and of course, we both get carded. I look eighteen, and Natalie acts like she's fifteen—though to be fair, no one would mistake her for being too young if she didn't open her mouth. The guy gives me a suspicious squint, thinking my license is fake. Seems this outfit shaves a few years off.

"Twenty-three? Really?" the guy frowns.

"Yes, really. Hang on." I dig my wallet out of my purse and flash my FD identification. The official hat and uniform shirt make me look at least twenty. "See? I blame my good genes."

The bouncer takes my fire department ID and holds it close, comparing the pictures.

Irritated, I glare at him. "I am old enough."

He flinches, remains still for a second, and hands me back the IDs before speaking in a slow monotone. "You're old enough."

"Thanks." I nab the IDs and fumble to put them away. Way to get my night off on the right foot.

Natalie scurries up beside me. "Dude. Did you just mind-wank the bouncer?"

"Huh?"

She grins. "You like totally did. You said"—her voice drops, stinking at trying to imitate me—"I'm old enough. And he was all like zombie"—Natalie holds her arms out and moans—"You're old enough."

I laugh. "I can't do that kinda stuff. Only move things." Really. I can't. I peer back at the guy who's talking normally again. *Did* I do that, or was he messing with us?

She pulls me inside before I can think more about it. We pass a coat check area in a short hallway connecting the entrance to the main room. Black walls make it feel claustrophobic and narrow. I don't see any obvious exits other than the one we're in. Geez. I am sure glad I can't burn. This place would be a deathtrap if fire broke out.

Niflheim's interior has three distinct sections. All the way on the right, there's a stage and dance floor awash in flashing lights. A girl in a lame blonde wig dressed up like a techno-Valkyrie is doing the DJ thing on the stage, and there's so many people gyrating around that my 'fire code violation' sense is screaming.

Nothing like a responsible day job to suck the fun out of life.

The middle space, right in front of us, has a bunch of tiny, round tables at standing height. A crowd of twenty-somethings, about half Goths, mingle about, using the tables mostly to hold their drinks. Off to the left, the décor gives off a restaurant vibe, with bigger, normal-height tables and some booth seats. They took a page out of those kitschy places' book—there's crap all over the walls, but it's like axes, shields, swords, yeti-masks and such. Like if Vikings invaded a TGI Fridays.

"Where to?" I ask.

Natalie grins, grabs my hand, and drags me to the dance area.

Cool.

When we first started doing our semi-weekly 'outings,' the main plan had been to find guys to hook up with. Two years later, we go to have fun and unwind. I suppose if we happen to run into a pair of guys who get past my intuition—and by that, I mean reading their intentions—we might see where that takes us, but it's not like before. Back then, we had a pact that if one of us hooked up with a guy, and the other didn't, one of us would be cool going home alone. Nowadays, it's both or nothing. We're here for *us*.

The techno music is timed to the flashing lights. At least a third of the dancers on the floor wear Viking-y accessories. More than a few have plastic helmets. At least six are dressed like Goths, two of which have on fake horns. A couple even have vampire fangs. Never did understand that particular fetish.

Natalie and I start out dancing near each other, but as the crowd shifts and flows, we separate. Bodies bump and rub against each other. I get pawed a little, and paw right back. My hair's down to my waist and thick; it could hide the headband for those fake horns.

Did I mention I have shitty impulse control?

Before I can even try to do it on purpose, my horns pop out. Amid the flashing colored lights, the gyrating bodies, and the overall dimness, they become another piece of costume fantasy. The music gets into my blood, and I throw myself into the spinning dance.

Minutes later, my mojo's interrupted when a guy slides his hand around my waist and pulls me in close, chest to chest. Oh what the hell? I snarl playfully at him while we undulate together.

"Awesome fangs," he yells over the music.

Oops. Wow, I have fangs too? I feel my eyes widen, but I laugh. "You say the sweetest things."

"Where'd you get 'em? They're badass. So real looking." He half-turns away, his body twisting and bending in time with the music.

"My mother gave them to me." So, I'm being a wiseass; he doesn't need to know that.

"Right on. Your mom sounds cool."

I grin. Yeah, she is. Okay, now I *know* I'm old. Mom and I never really fought, even at my worst. Nor did I ever 'hate' her. I spent a good few years thinking her an annoying killjoy, but seeing as how I can look at people and know their true intentions, I never doubted she loved me to the point of devotion. Really, the woman would've jumped into traffic to save me. It's really hard—even as a tween—to shout 'I hate you' after being grounded, when the person I'm about to bite the head off of is standing there radiating love and worry.

I'm glad she got away from that damn waitress job. She found a book some guy left behind in his seat that had a bunch of magic type stuff in it. Turns out, Mom had a gift. Not everyone can do magic—only about one in every couple hundred. Of that group, about three percent have serious ability, like tossing around fireballs or being a Lifemage, Hydromancer, or something that gets on TV.

Mom's in the first group, but she's pretty strong in divination. Once she got the hang of it, she started doing the fortuneteller bit, but before long, she wrote a book on mysticism and self-published it. The thing sold enough to become addictive, so she kept going.

She mostly writes mystical things, interpretations of visions or candle magic, but she's also putting out a fiction series. No one will accuse her of being rich, but she lives okay off it, and she doesn't get bitched at by people for undercooked meals anymore.

After wandering away from the guy, I put my sharps away and roam the dance floor until bumping into Natalie. She's had her fill of it too, so we head over to the restaurant section.

On the way across the space with the tall tables, an odd feeling pulls my attention to the bar at my right. The bartender's over six feet tall with broad shoulders. His tight, pale grey t-shirt doesn't do much to conceal the shape of his prominent musculature. Mind you, he doesn't look like an overinflated pool float, so I doubt he's using steroids. The boy's not *too* big, but he's impressive. Straight blond hair frames a handsome, chiseled face that makes me think of an elf from a fantasy movie, but he's far too buff for that, and his ears have no points. Oddest of all, when I stare at him, I get nothing. No sense of intention whatsoever. That's never happened before, and I don't like it.

The man gives me a little nod as if to say, 'hey, what's up?' Like he recognizes me or something.

I return the gesture and hurry after Nat to a table. For the first time in my life, I suppress one of my sudden urges—to tell her about what's happening with me. Maybe she'd know what I am or if I've been cursed. But this goes beyond the 'oh, by the way, I like girls' kind of conversation. You think you know someone and... they're gay. From her, I'd expect a 'oh, hey that's cool' and we'd go right back into whatever other topic we'd been discussing. Somehow, I think 'oh, by the way, I'm a demon' would get a different response.

Maybe.

I've known her for five years. Second to Mom, she's the person I trust the most.

She's also an enchanter, and a decently skilled one at that. Magic works different ways for different people. Lifemages, for example, can channel magic until they pass out from the effort, and they'll never create fire. Likewise, elementalists can strain until they crap their pants and they'll never heal even a paper cut. Hydromancers have command over water and ice-based spells, but no matter how much they study, they'll never make lightning or fire.

I have to tell her... but I can put it off until after I get a chance to talk to my mother.

"The bartender's all about you, girl," says Natalie. "I bet the guy's had some cosmetic enchants. No one is *that* perfect without help."

A girl our age in dark tights and a purple t-shirt with the word 'Niflheim' over a battleax walks up to our table. Her shirt matches the colored streaks in her otherwise-black hair. "Hey. I'm Jen. I'll be taking care of you tonight. Can I start you off with something to drink?"

"Uhh, Cherry Shift for me," says Natalie.

"I'll go for a Steve Adams. Whatever's on tap."

"Gotcha." Jen grins at us and zips off.

Natalie notices my smirk and leans close. "What?"

"Why do you waste money on that stuff? What's the point of drinking soda if it disappears?"

"Brook!" She giggles. "Were you drunk or stoned last time?"

I shrug. "Flip a coin."

We both laugh. In truth, I can't recall ever being so far gone I lost track of myself. I've been drunk, and I've been high on various things, but I got bored with it before eighteen. For one thing, it takes a shitload of alcohol (or weed) to get me stumbling, and it got expensive. For another, if I want to stay with the fire department, I can't test positive for drugs. I figure the amount of experimentation that went on from sixteen to eighteen got it out of my system.

And by the way, peyote is some *wild* shit.

"I explained it already." She swats her hand at me.

"So you did. I forgot, or I wasn't paying attention. Don't worry about it." I glance at the bar. The Viking warrior god is—"He's still looking at me."

"It doesn't disappear. It's called 'shift' because it turns into water after you drink it. No calories, no chemicals. The bubbles and flavor are illusions." Natalie grins. "I love magic. Wait, he what?" She spins in her seat to peer at the bar. As if he expected her to, the man turns to a guy ordering a drink a second before her gaze finds him. "He turned away, didn't he?"

"Yeah."

Jen comes back and sets our drinks down. I got a bog-standard beer, but Natalie's fizzy red concoction is glowing. The cherry flavor is so damn strong I can taste it in the air. "Do you guys need a minute?"

"Nah, I'm good." I grab one of the menus from a cubby on the left side of our booth, and order the first thing my gaze falls on. "Can I get the rib tips, please?"

"You get two sides with that," says Jen.

"Right… garlic mash and the house salad."

Natalie studies the menu until Jen's about to offer us more time to think, but she goes for boneless hot wings plus fries and a Caesar.

I tell her about the fire Wednesday, which grabs her undivided attention for most of the time we spend waiting for our meal. I leave out my change—for now—replacing the story with the ceiling falling in and 'nearly missing' us before we scrambled down a stairwell. The whole time, that bartender is giving me the eye. I *hate* not being able to tell what he's planning. I pretty much suck at reading body language since I've spent my whole life simply knowing people at a look.

The reads don't lift secrets. I can't like dive into someone's head and dig out their email password, but if a guy really loves cats, or if a big scary biker's a softie at heart, yeah, can't hide that. Also, if the harmless looking guy who seems friendly to everyone is really on the hunt for a little girl to grab, I read that shit like a damn book. Maybe that experience *did* traumatize me. I keep wanting to kill that guy over again.

My secret admirer behind the bar's got a raised eyebrow the next time I look at him. Did someone nearby say something he didn't expect? My sense of unease worsens.

"Are you sure you don't want to do something safer? Good grief, Brooklyn, you could've died!" Natalie reaches across the table and grabs my hand.

I give her my best reassuring smile. "I'm fine. It's my calling. You know, the trailer. Feels like the universe let me slide away from death, and working this job is how I pay it back, helping others."

"That's like really deep." She sighs, smiling. "Oh, hey, I make baubles."

"You make *expensive* baubles." I wink. "How's the shop doing?"

"Oh, a little slow. Only had three enchants last month." She rests her elbows on the table and leans her chin on both hands, making a face like a little girl who'd been denied a pony for her birthday.

"Didn't you tell me once that if you made ten enchants in a year, you could pay rent and not worry about food?"

"Yeah," she whines. "It's not the money. It's *fun*. The ideas my customers come up with to request are never the same. It's a challenge to figure out how to make magic do what they like. I hate sitting around watching dust build up on my shelves."

You could make me a shirt that lets my wings out without shredding off me. I purse my lips in thought. I'd ask, but I can't afford her. Something like that would probably be a couple grand. Of course, the shirt would become indestructible and never need to be washed. Maybe if I get rich, and stop being a coward. I'd kinda have to tell her about my having extra body parts.

The bartender's stare drills into my skull like an annoyingly bright sun that keeps getting in my eyes, and this table has no shade to offer. At least when our food comes out, I have an excuse to focus my attention on something specific. While we eat, Natalie describes her most recent enchant, basically a flying Roomba that wields a featherduster. Exciting.

We decline dessert, but get coffee. Mr. Perfect continues watching me. He's either an ex-cop who thinks I'm still a terror, or he's sizing me up for a chloroform-soaked rag as soon as we leave. Maybe he hates Goths. I'm so pale, I 'goth' without even trying. Sometimes I get attitude for the way I look. Sometimes, idiots really need to mind their own damn business.

"You about ready?" I ask.

Natalie nods. "Wanna hit the floor again?"

"I'm stuffed. I'd throw up all over everyone if I tried to dance."

She sticks her tongue out. "Yuck. I'm guessing you don't feel like grabbing some shots at the bar?"

"Nah. Creep alert. I'm feeling kinda introverty tonight. How about my sofa? Movie?"

"Aww." She holds my hand again. "Is it the fire? And sure. Whatever you want."

I shake my head. "No, it's not the fire. This place is making me uncomfortable."

"It's the way that guy's staring at you, isn't it?" She glances over her shoulder at him, but again, he's already doing something else by the time she looks.

"Yep."

She scoots out of her seat. "Okay. Your place."

"Wait. We haven't paid." I reach for my AATM crystal.

"Put that thing away." She winks. "I picked this place; it's my turn. Wheel of food, remember?"

Right. We rotate who pays as well. Unless we screw up and stumble on a place that turns out to be way more expensive than we thought. Then we split it.

After a few awkward minutes of standing under the bartender's piercing gaze, I spot Jen bopping around at the back corner, chatting with three other employees. I stare at the side of her head, wanting her to get over here.

She stops talking mid-sentence, and looks toward me.

Whoa. Did I actually do something or was that a freakish coincidence?

I smile and wave at her.

Jen's expression goes apologetic. She darts out from behind the servers' station and runs over to us. "I'm *so* sorry about that. I could've sworn you guys had left already."

"It's okay." Natalie smiles. "We needed a few minutes to let the food settle."

"I feel bad about making you wait." Jen takes Natalie's AATM crystal and plugs it into a combination reader hanging from her belt that also takes magnetic cards for the 'magic averse' crowd.

Natalie puts her thumb on the crystal and uses her finger to write on an illusory document, adding a huge twenty-five dollar tip.

"Thank you so much; you guys were great!" Jen looks ready to hug us, but only smiles.

I grab Nat by the arm and drag her to the door. The last time I wanted to get the hell out of somewhere this bad, I'd been in jail. Hey, jail is scary for an eleven-year-old. Even a cell in a tiny local police station. I'd been stuck there for one day as an 'object lesson.' Not that I'd ever have admitted it at the time, but those twenty-six or so hours had been utterly terrifying. 'Course, as soon as they brought me to my mother in the lobby, 'tough girl' came back. Mom knew though. She saw the fear in my eyes as soon as we were in the car. And, okay, maybe I did cry a little when she hugged me. I tried to act brave and said at least she didn't have to worry about a babysitter. Maybe that's why she let the cops keep me all weekend two years later.

"That guy was ridiculously good looking," says Natalie as she flops on my sofa.

"He creeped me the hell out. I don't like being stared at the way a guy stares at steak." I toss her the remote on my way to the bedroom. "Pick a movie. I'm gonna get comfortable."

"'Kay."

After I change, I glide back into the living room in a long t-shirt and sweatpants, mercifully free of underwear or shoes. Natalie's got her heels off and stoops forward while sitting cross-legged on the sofa. My TV emits a constant *ping, ping, ping* from her scrolling across movie titles. I keep going right past her and enter the kitchen, where I open the cabinet and stare at my popcorn stash.

"Butter or cheese?" I yell.

"Sounds like a personal problem."

"Popcorn, dumbass."

She laughs. "I don't care."

I toss a pack of 'butter flavor' popcorn into the rune oven. Twenty seconds on blue should be perfect. The constant chiming from the living room continues, louder than the thrum of the blue energy stream hitting the popcorn packet. After nineteen seconds, a brilliant flash fills the oven and the bag inflates in an instant.

Buttery goodness fills the air.

Awesome. Didn't turn into cherry-banana this time.

Speaking of which, I really need to complain to the superin—"Hey, Nat?"

The pinging stops. "Yeah?"

"How good are you with rune ovens? Can you fix someone else's enchantment?"

"Oh, those things are so cheap." She rolls her eyes in contempt. "One 'chanter who's way over his school spreading a low-grade spell over fifty blanks at once."

Bowl tucked under my left arm, I wander to the opening connecting my kitchen to the living room, lean on the frame, and munch. "I have no damn idea what you just said."

She uncrosses her legs and looks at me. "Okay, you know magic is rated in schools, right?"

"Yeah, beginner, novice, acolyte, that sorta thing."

"Okay, so if you have someone who's like, oh, Second Order tossing an acolyte level spell, they can add more power to it. They use a diffusion crystal to spread an enchantment that's supposed to affect one item, or blank, to work on twenty or more at a time." She waves dismissively while rolling her eyes again. "It's *so* annoying. Zero respect for the craft."

I sit beside her and offer the bowl. "So you're saying you either can't fix it, or it's so far beneath you that you'll feel dirty for touching it."

"Yeah, basically." She grabs a handful of popcorn, grinning. "I'll check it out before I go, and if it's in bad shape, I'll make you a real one."

"Nat, you know I can't afford custom 'chants."

She pauses mid-munch, eyeing me sideways. "I'm kinda hurt you'd think I would charge you. It's not even a complex spell."

"I didn't mean that... I mean I didn't want to assume you'd work for free." I press a fist to her shoulder and give her a light push. "I respect what you do too much."

Natalie's wounded expression fades. "Okay. You can pay me back by letting me study you a bit."

Popcorn gets stuck in my throat as I cough. She swats my back a few times, hovering over me. Great. I survive a massive hotel fire and die to a piece of junk food wedged in my trachea. My eyes water, but I manage to hack it up before suffering permanent brain damage from oxygen deprivation.

"Whoa. You okay?" She keeps rubbing my back.

"Yeah." A few deep breaths later, I blink away the tears and exhale hard. "Wow, that hurt. Umm, what do you mean by 'study me?'"

"Remember a couple months ago how that Aznian crystal in my shop glowed crimson when you touched it? I still haven't been able to figure out what that means." Natalie shrinks in on herself, widening her eyes and holding her hands together at her chin. Her voice shifts pitch to that of a little girl. "I really kinda want to."

Oh, whew. She didn't notice my horns. I think I've discovered *why* it glowed, but not what it means. I'm going to tell her eventually, but not yet. "Sure. As long as whatever you're going to do to me doesn't involve body parts disappearing or appearing."

Oh, wow. I could *so* mess with her. I grin at the thought.

"Done." She pops up and thrusts her hand out to shake.

I grab it. "So, pick a movie yet?"

"No. I've either seen all these or they look stupid. Why aren't there any decent ones here?"

"Streaming." I shrug. "Gotta sign up for the physical crystals to get the good movies."

"Ugh." Natalie shakes her head. "Physical crystals for movies? Seriously? *Hello*, everyone's got high-speed Aethernet. What century are we in?"

We finish the popcorn before a movie is chosen. No sooner do I get up to make another pack than she yells in victory.

"Aha! Got one." She points at a 'haunted mansion' type title. The cover art looks creepy as hell, some guy stretching into a warped/ghostly image.

"You sure? The last flick like that we watched, you hid behind me for most of it." I laugh all the way to the kitchen.

"But you're big and strong," She fake-mewls before laughing.

I zap another bag of popcorn and dump it in the bowl. As I'm returning to the living room, Tracy and Frank start going at it again. Shouting, with the occasional *thud* of something thrown across the room. Great.

Natalie stares at the wall on the left. "This happen a lot?"

I plop down beside her, set the bowl on the sofa between us, and hit play. "Yeah, three, four nights a week. On a good week."

Frank gets stuck repeating 'stupid bitch' with the occasional c bomb thrown in. Whatever Tracy's screaming back at him is too distorted to make out words. Natalie flinches at every *thud, crash, or slam.*

"Damn, Brook... you should complain to the building manager. How can you stand living next to that?"

Feet on the coffee table, I scoot back into the sofa with a pillow clutched to my chest. "Won't help. The manager's not exactly responsive. Sometimes I swear he's a construct."

She gives me the side eye again. "They stuck you with a golem for a super? That's illegal."

I laugh. "No. He's got the personality of one, and about the same amount of thinking capacity."

Frank bellows loud and long for another few seconds before lowering his volume to the point only a continuous murmur leaks through the wall. Why is she still with that moron? This is why I'm still single. Well, that, and being able to know a guy's intentions. Occasionally, I hook up with one of the 'just wants to get in my pants' types for some no-strings fun. Hey, a girl's got needs, right? Anyone who's looking for a possession or a servant? No thanks.

"I should make something calming." Natalie grins at me. "Give it to them like as a 'welcome to the building' present. Once it's in their space, it'll keep their moods level."

"Hah." I laugh. "I don't think your magic's strong enough for that douche. Your charm token would overheat."

She raspberries me. "I'm gonna enchant some damn silence over them if they don't knock it off."

Two can play that game. Sorta. I turn up the volume. The apartment on my right side is still—as far as I know—empty. "Tracy and Frank are going to join us for the movie... only without being able to see it."

"Ooh." She narrows her eyes at me, grinning. "You're evil."

"Nah. I'm merely misunderstood." I wink.

6

UNUSUAL CIRCUMSTANCES

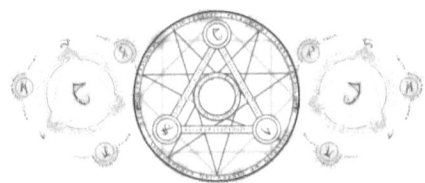

Thursday of the following week, my stationhouse responded to a blaze at a medium-sized restaurant. By the time we got there, the building had already advanced to the 'lost-cause' state. Fire roared inside like a bunch of elementals having a bachelor party at a place with an open bar. Flames and smoke belched out of the windows, and half the roof had already collapsed. If there'd been anyone inside, they'd already have been quite well done.

Word came back that they hadn't opened for the day yet, meaning the only people who could've been inside would be burglars or arsonists. So, we got ordered to work containment, keeping the flames from spreading. Only one Hydromancer showed up since the scene didn't trip as many stations as the hotel had. She put a water bubble over the whole thing to protect surrounding properties while the rest of us did things the usual way, with hoses. We threw water on it, but really, as far gone as it was, everyone knew we mostly intended to let it burn itself out.

It's a long, sweaty, messy afternoon.

Once the joint is a huge pile of smoking ashes, I get stuck rolling up the hoses again. Some of the guys still give me shit for being a woman. I don't even need to read their intention: they're hoping it's too much for little ol' me and I go whining and crying to the lieutenant or someone higher up the food chain. They'd find it funny to watch 'the girl' cry. I still don't get why they think this is so difficult. Tedious, yes. Ass-busting? No.

I glance down at the bundle of hose over my shoulder that I'm carrying to the truck. Hmm. They always look at me weird, like they're waiting for something. It occurs to me as I heave the first bundle into the back that I've seen the guys grunt doing this. Dunn had trouble with the hotel door that I kicked clear in. And Lamar. I did throw him straight out of his chair when we arm-wrestled.

Wings. Horns. Huh. Maybe I *am* way stronger than a woman my size ought to be. That would certainly explain a few things... like Vince Milligan. Who's that? Oh, just some kid I kicked in the balls in fifth grade. He'd been teasing me all year for being poor. When I ignored that, he picked on me for being too pale. Which, well, I was, so... whatever. The asshole pissed me off when he started saying shit about my mom, so I pushed him and told him to shut up. He hit me, like straight up fist-to-the-face hit me. Everyone watching us gasped that he'd legit slugged a girl smaller than him. Looked worse than it was. I don't remember it hurting much at all, but it *did* make me see red. At that age, what did I know about fighting? First thing that came to mind—punt him where it hurts most.

He crumpled straight to the ground and didn't get up. Wow, did he scream.

Fortunately, enough of our classmates (and a teacher) saw him nail me in the nose first that I didn't get expelled, but Vince never came back. He transferred to a private school after he got out of the hospital. Rumor went around that I'd cracked his pelvis. From that day onward, everyone left me alone or avoided me, which suited me fine.

I'm on all fours atop the truck putting the sixth hose away when a man's voice comes from behind me.

"Hey, need a hand?"

I look back at Jason Dunn. He's pale too, being a ginger, but not to the point of a freak like me. "Hey. I thought this was women's work?"

"Ehh, don't mind those guys. They're too dense to understand you don't let them get to you." He tosses a hose up.

"Dense, yeah." I catch it and slide it in place. "That's one way to call it."

He laughs and wanders off to get the next hose. I hop down and start rolling another from where the guys had laid them all out straight to drain. While bundling it up, a shimmer to the right grabs my eye. A spot among the wet, smoldering ash emits a weak, but noticeable purplish glow.

Okay, that's not reflected sun.

"Hang on a sec. Be right back," I say, before leaving the half-rolled hose and crossing the parking lot to the edge of what had once been an up-and-coming bistro.

A ragged trace of the outer wall remains surrounding heaps of smoking debris, making the former restaurant resemble a giant ashtray. My gaze fixed on the glowing spot, I step over a low part of the wall and navigate my way inside.

"Hey," calls an older man. "Hold on. We haven't been in there yet."

I stop two paces from the wall and spin to face a guy with wild, white hair rushing over. He's in a dress uniform—white shirt, black pants—and has lieutenant's insignia on his shoulders. He outranks me (and his tone is more requesting than ordering), so I wait.

"Amari?" he asks, once he's close enough to read the black letters on the reflective yellow tag across my coat. "You got a reason for going back in? Trying to keep tromping to a minimum so we can get a proper investigation done."

His lieutenant's pins have a little red star in them, and he's got a Fire Marshal's Office ribbon. If he's from the FMO, he's arson investigation. His nametag reads *Hilleman. J.*

"I thought I saw something strange. Something you guys might want to take a look at."

Hilleman leans on the wall and peers past me. "I don't see anything. What caught your eye?"

"I'm not sure. A glint of purple light. Give me a moment, and I'll tell you more." I pick my way through the ash without waiting for permission. Hey, easier to ask for forgiveness, right? "It's just over here.

To my surprise, Hilleman doesn't rip my head off. He hurries off to the side to enter via a gap that used to be a doorway. Guess if I had on dress slacks, I wouldn't want to crawl over a half-burned wall either. I set my boots with care, trying to not fall on my ass while making at least some effort to minimize disruption.

Hilleman follows me to the spot where the light is still shimmering. He doesn't notice it until we're three steps away, at which point he lets out an, "Oh, that!? How on Earth did you catch that from all the way back there?" He gestures at where Dunn is still rolling hose. "I'm not sure I'd have seen that if you hadn't led me right to it."

"Lucky, I guess?" I squat nearby and brush my gloved fingers over the ash pile, exposing an amethyst crystal about the size of a chickpea. "Crystal of some kind."

He stoops, squinting at it. "Could be a bauble someone dropped."

"Could be." Random dropped jewelry doesn't tend to glow. At least not usually. I pull my glove off and grasp the crystal.

The second my fingers touch it, an explosion of phantasmal light surrounds me. I tend to react to being startled by going statue still. Spectral men and women, walls, and tables recreate the restaurant that had been—up until a few hours ago—standing here. I find myself squatting in a ghostly shadow of the past. Waiters and waitresses walk by in the aisle. Diners at other tables seem to be talking but make no sound. Everything is transparent and washed out, all the color muted to an odd sepia tone—except for one man.

My point of view is a little above and behind him. His hair is black with more than a few greys, and he's got it combed back into a helmet that could deflect bullets. In the midst of picking at what appears to be some manner of pasta-and-shrimp dish, he takes the crystal out of his pocket and affixes it to the bottom of his table with two-sided tape. No one seems to notice.

In an instant, everyone vanishes. I get the feeling time has gone forward by several hours. My point of view is at the level of a toddler, below the tables. The crystal, still stuck in place, emits a brilliant red flash. Serpents of flame go in all directions. For the second time in minutes, I'm startled enough for my muscles to lock up.

The vision fades, leaving me staring down at shiny, black shoes. Hands squeeze my shoulders, holding me upright.

"—medical crew over here," yells Hilleman.

"Huh?" I look up at the lieutenant who's squatting in front of me, gripping me by the shoulders. "What?"

"Are you all right, Amari?" asks Hilleman. "You lost consciousness."

"I'm okay." I hold up the crystal. "I think I just had... I don't know... a vision?"

He raises an eyebrow.

I explain what I saw. "I watched the man plant the crystal. This is what started the fire."

Hilleman's face collapses into an expression like I told him he needed to audit 30,000 reports.

When I glance down again at the crystal, my mind fills with the image of a smiling older woman. Her pewter hair hangs shoulder-length, and her glasses have faeries built into the frames on either side. A strong feeling of positive energy washes over me. That woman liked this crystal. A lot. Almost as if she regarded it as a living pet.

"Whoa," I say.

"What?" Hilleman stops massaging the bridge of his nose and stares at me. "There's more?"

"Think I saw the person the firebug bought the crystal from." I offer it up to him. "Guess this is yours now, for the investigation."

Hilleman groans. "Ugh. Magic. Why do I have a sinking feeling we're not going to find any accelerants when we do the testing?" He holds the crystal in his palm, glaring at it. "Amari, how would you feel about assisting in this investigation? It's a bit outside our usual scope. We could use a psychic."

"I'm not..." I blink. "Okay, maybe I am. This is the first time I've ever had one of those... uhh, visions. Don't you guys have a magic division?"

"Well, we did have a guy, but…" Hilleman blanches. "The umm, position's still vacant. Hang around for a little bit, will you?"

"Sure Ell-tee." I shrug and make my way back to the engine, but Dunn's already got the hoses away.

He smiles, leaning against the back end. "I'd be annoyed you were gone so long, but you did get most of it done before I volunteered. What'cha talkin' to the FM about?"

"Oh, saw something in the ash." I sit on the bumper and explain what happened.

Dunn lowers himself next to me, legs wide, holding his helmet between his knees. "So you're psychic, too?"

Oh my. He's crushing on me. It's shining off him like a three-alarm fire at a propane bottling plant. This is a legitimately new experience for me. I've read curiosity on the first couple of boys I kissed, and a whole bunch of 'let's do it' on the ones that followed. Never before have I felt like a guy wanted like a relationship or something beyond jumping to the sex part as fast as possible. I suppose some of that is my fault for being the 'bad girl' during school. Most of the nice guy types steered well away from me, and it's not like I went out of my way to socialize.

"Yeah, I guess I am. Always had been. In a different way, though."

He grins. "Oh? Like you can read minds?"

"Not really." I stare at my hands, fidgeting with the gloves I'm holding. "More like I can look at people and understand what their overall mindset is, what they're intent on doing in the moment… sometimes what kind of person they are."

His body stiffens. "So—"

"What are your intentions?" I turn the bundle of gloves over and over. "You're circling around, feeling me out, hoping I'm receptive to being asked on a date. And I think you're also hoping for something a little more than a hook up."

Dunn is done. He sputters, chuckles a little, and stares at me with abject worry.

"I think it's cute. Though, I must admit that's not the reaction I was expecting when you, uhh, saw me the other day." I look up, finally making eye contact. "That… other stuff doesn't bother you?"

"Umm." He lets his helmet dangle by its strap over one finger. "You know, I've been wondering myself why it doesn't. One of my friends is seeing a woman with pointy ears."

"Elves aren't real."

"Oh, of course not." He chuckles. "She had them modified by a Lifemage. I know you're the psychic one and all, but last week… I've never had someone really care about me that much before, whether I lived or died. I never even thought about the… wings and stuff. I mean, you didn't even know you could shrug off a backdraft like that, and you still refused to leave me there."

I shrug. "Fire never scared me. In fact, it has the reverse effect. I find it comforting."

"That's cool." He twists his helmet back and forth.

"No…" I lean against him, head on his shoulder, and tilt my head so we make eye contact. "Fire is warm, not cool."

He laughs.

"Give it a couple days, and if you still want to ask me out on a date, I'll accept." I sit up straight and smile at him.

He stares at me quizzically. "Couple days?"

Hilleman, plus two other men, an older guy with a grey flat-top afro and a mid-thirties white dude carrying a suitcase cross the parking lot toward us.

"Yep." I stand. "I can see your intent, but not the why of it. I'm asking you to let things settle in your head and make sure the way you're feeling right now isn't some reaction to what happened. I'm… intrigued by all this, but I don't want you to get pulled into a relationship that won't work because you've convinced yourself that you owe me."

He stands and leans close. "I can see that, but it's not only because you saved my ass."

Hilleman and the other two stop a few paces away.

I wink and give him my number. "Looks like I gotta go."

Dunn digs his phone out from under all his gear and adds me to his contacts. "Got it. Call you... tomorrow?"

"That works," I say.

Grinning, he wanders off to finish helping with the cleanup.

I approach the three FMs.

"Amari, this is Lawrence Ellis"—the guy with the grey afro nods—"and Paul Hayden."

The guy with the case flashes a weary smile. "I couldn't find anything on that little crystal you found."

"It's arcane," says Ellis. "Clearly."

"No accelerants in there." Hayden pats his equipment. "Beyond the oil from the kitchen. Based on the burn pattern, the fire started at twelve different places with an extreme amount of heat, but there's no detectable cause of ignition."

Hilleman shakes his head while sighing out his nose. "It's usually like that when magic gets involved. Look, Amari, we'd like you to help out with this investigation. You've got a good eye and a good instinct about fire."

He doesn't want to deal with it. Doesn't even like that his team has to juggle this. I can tell he's not hoping for failure, but he's not a fan of magic. Wants nothing to do with it. I did something supernatural, so I'm a giant friggin' guinea pig he can offload this on.

"How does that work?" I ask.

"I've already spoken to Captain Greene. She's in charge of the arson investigation unit of the Fire Marshall's Office. In turn, she's spoken with Lieutenant Sims. For the duration of this investigation, you'd be temporarily attached to the FMO and would be working with Lieutenant Ellis here."

Lieutenant Ellis chuckles. "Please, call me Lawrence."

"Assuming, of course, you're interested," adds Hilleman.

Being 'in the shit' is an allure that I find difficult to shake, but this also sounds fascinating. And it's not like he's offering a permanent transfer or anything. Why not? This could be fun.

"Sure," I say.

Lawrence checks his watch. Wow. I didn't think anyone still had one of those in the smartphone era. "How confident are you that the crystal's the source? Do you think there's anything else in there we missed?"

"Pretty sure, but I can check around again, see if I notice anything else."

"All right. Let's give it another walkthrough. After that, why don't you go clean up and switch to the polo and we can try and figure out where to go from here."

Natalie comes to mind.

I wink and start walking toward the burned ruin. "I've got an idea already, once we're done here."

7

ENCHANTED EVENINGS

O ver the next few hours, I roam the burned-out restaurant with Lawrence. He shows me the spots where they believe ignition occurred, though at this point, their theory that the fire started in twelve different places is based on the spread of the burn pattern on the ground. The fire had been so hot, little of the interior structure remains. It's difficult to even identify where the boundaries between various rooms had been. Nothing else draws my attention, and by the time we leave, the rest of the fire crew is long gone.

He gives me a ride back to my stationhouse in a red SUV labeled *Fire Marshal.* After a quick shower and change to a fresh uniform (a white polo shirt with FD markings and black BDU pants), I hurry outside and climb into his truck.

While we'd been snooping around for any additional clues, I'd mentioned Natalie. He liked the idea, so he'd agreed to let her have a look at the crystal once I'd changed. The shower leaves me smelling only a *little* like an ashtray. I feel almost official or something, going out in public in this uniform. Normally, it's hidden under an extra set of flame-retardant pants and a big coat plus air tank.

"Here." Lawrence hands me a nametag that reads *assistant arson investigator*.

I take it and pin it on my shirt. "Thanks. Guess if I need to project authority, it'll help."

He chuckles.

A short drive later, we pull up and park in front of Natalie's shop, 'Enchanted Evenings,' in Kensington. It's a short walk away from a little hole-in-the-wall called 'Reanimator Coffee' in a weird pie-slice shaped building. I always stop in there whenever I visit Nat. I love the high-octane stuff. Wonder if Lawrence likes java?

Natalie's window is a diorama with ten-inch dolls reenacting a scene from some Victorian romance. The door opens on its own—without electronics—and a diaphanous wind-chime sound peals over the room. It's not a huge place; two rows of shelves go down the middle of the rectangular store full of 'pre-made' enchanted items that have a good chance of selling. Stink-less ashtrays, ever-sharp kitchen knives, permanent air fresheners, that sort of thing. Two bookshelves hem in the area right behind the front window, creating a small playroom for kids, where she's got a handful of enchanted toys on display. A wooden train set chugs around a wooden track, an illusion of smoke trailing off its chimney.

At the gentle *pop* of the door closing, my friend pokes her head up from behind the counter, wearing an eager, happy expression and a plain blue dress. As soon as she spots me, the eagerness falls away. Alas, I'm not a customer about to drop ten grand on a vacuum cleaner that can talk or a set of undirtiable dishes that put themselves away.

Most of her enchants are quite utilitarian, but she's made good money from the city for beefing up the police's armored vests.

"Hey, Nat." I walk up to the glass counter; the top shelf inside is full of wands. "Oh wow, you still have those?"

"Yeah, that idiot senator's bill failed." She huffs, making her bangs jump. A pendant around her neck, a silver witch sitting on a crescent moon, comes to life and waves at me. "They're not treating them like guns yet, so I can still sell them." Her gaze shifts to Lawrence. "Who's that?"

"Lieutenant Ellis from the Fire Marshal's Office, arson investigation's unit," I say.

He offers a hand. "Please, Lawrence is fine. A pleasure to meet you."

She accepts, shaking his hand with far more vigor than he expected, making his eyebrows go up.

I feel like a ghost. Lawrence is dark, and Natalie's got this rich caramel color to her skin. I could trip into a snowbank and disappear. I've never been a vain person, but after realizing that I might not even be human, the difference feels more like a blinking neon sign calling attention to my 'otherness.'

"So, what's up?" asks Natalie.

Lawrence pulls a small black jeweler's box from his pocket and sets it on the counter. "Your friend thinks this crystal is involved in a fire we're investigating. We have questions and no answers to go with them."

"Oh, cool." Natalie picks up the box, but hesitates. "I mean, not cool that something burned, but cool you're asking me to help."

I lean on the counter. "And I'm part of the investigation now because I found it."

"What are you leaving out?" Natalie gives me a playful grin and opens the little box. "Oh, hello. Poor little guy. He's all dwained and tired."

My eyebrows furrow. "Do you always baby talk at things?"

"Not everything." Natalie holds up the crystal. "This little guy's cute."

It's a lump of lavender-hued crystal. No idea how she gets 'cute' from that. Kittens are cute. Baby seals are cute. Babies are cute (until they throw up on me). They're little Winston Churchills that explode if shaken. Crystals? Whatever.

She stares at it, holding it up to the light. "So what aren't you telling me?"

I explain the vision I got.

"Oh wow." Natalie lowers her arm and switches her gawking from the crystal to me. "You're a clairvoyant, too? When did that start?"

"This afternoon," I deadpan, folding my arms.

She pulls out a notepad and scribbles a few lines. "That's something I need to add to my research. If you're able to get psychometric visions, that could open a whole new path we need to walk down."

"Psycho-what?" I blink.

She sighs. "Of course the person who can do it is the one who doesn't understand it."

"I've never done it before a few hours ago. I didn't even want to. Just touched the crystal and whammo."

"Right," says Natalie. "From what I've read about them, people who can get psychometric visions usually receive them at a subconscious level when handling objects that have been exposed to high levels of emotional, spiritual, or magical energy. Maybe you've never touched anything with enough mojo in it before."

I shrug. "Maybe."

"Can she do this whenever she wants to, or only randomly?" asks Lawrence.

"I'm an enchanter, not a psychic. I only read a lot. But, I think if she practices at it, she'll get some control." Natalie sets the crystal down on the counter and holds her hands out over it. She intones a few indecipherable words definitely not in English, or Spanish, or even Swahili. A pair of concentric circles of orange light appear over the crystal, about four inches apart. Mystical symbols fill in the space between the rings, and hair-thin threads of energy wisp from the emptiness in the middle to the crystal.

Lawrence stands still and quiet, one eyebrow raised.

This trick, I've seen before. She's 'reading' the item. The spell she used should tell her exactly what it is, assuming it's enchanted.

"Oh, it's a spellstore." At a quick little finger motion from Natalie, the glowing sigil she made disappears. "It's got a twelve-thread capacity and a somewhat dangerous sub-enchant. At first, I thought it a ridiculous thing to even do, but it makes sense given how you found it."

Lawrence leans in close, pulling out a notepad. "Go on."

"Dangerous? I guess you could say burning a place to the ground is dangerous." I set my hands on my hips.

"I can see the last magic someone put into this thing." Natalie eyes Lawrence. "Your friend looks like he doesn't know magic from a double-caramel latte."

"Not the least bit." He grins.

"Okay. A spellstore is an enchanted item that a mage can cast magic into, and it holds it. Later, the object can be invoked, and the spell proceeds," says Natalie.

Lawrence jots, while nodding.

"Every aspect of a spell is based on threads. If a spell does two things, it has two arcane threads running it. Like a spell that makes light. If that light is also capable of following its creator around, the motion part is a second thread." Natalie picks up the crystal. "This is a pretty advanced spellstore, and also rare Dragon Quartz."

"Valuable?" I ask.

"Not for being a gem. It's still basically quartz." She waves it at me. "Like different metals conduct electricity better, different crystals, metals, and gems absorb magic at varying degrees. Dragon Quartz is close to perfect, even as a semiprecious stone. You don't really get better than this unless you get into expensive stuff like rubies, sapphires, or diamonds."

"Are there 'Dragon Diamonds,' too?" asks Lawrence.

I hold up a hand, smiling. "Don't get her started, or we'll be here until tomorrow."

She shoots me a 'go to heck' look before leaning toward Lawrence. "Yes, there are. 'Dragon' only means the gem/crystal/rock/whatever has been exposed to magical energies over long periods, usually from being in rocks sitting on ley lines. It's got nothing to do with actual dragons. Anyway, so I don't 'keep you here all day'"—she sticks her tongue out at me—"the last magic inside this crystal was twelve single-thread fire spells."

"I'm shocked," I say.

Lawrence chuckles.

"Magic fire is hotter than normal fire, right?" I ask. "I kinda remember that. The place was a damn cinder before we even got there."

"Yep." She nods. "The spells put in this one were combat magic. Most non-wizards call them 'firebolts.' They're quite a bit hotter than ambient, natural fire. They only last for a second or three at most, and a single one has been known to kill people."

"Hmm." I tap my fingers on the counter. "The other investigators found twelve points where they think ignition occurred, and you're saying that crystal held twelve spells."

"Yep." She mutters two words in that indecipherable language again and pokes her finger at the air, making a glowing white dot. "Crystal here." One by one, she traces lines outward from it, like writing with glowing paint on a nonexistent piece of glass, each one radiating in a spiral until she's drawn a pinwheel. "Uncontained ray-type spells almost always curve. Left and high when north of the Equator, right and down if south. If you draw something like this over a blueprint of that restaurant that burned, I bet you'll connect to the locations where they think the fire started."

"Someone *really* wanted that little bistro gone," says Lawrence. "It's more common than you think for restaurants that aren't doing too well to have 'accidents.' Though, this goes a bit above and beyond the usual kitchen fire."

"What's the other part?" I gesture at the crystal. "You said something in it's dangerous?"

"Oh yeah." Natalie cringes. "I don't think this spellstore is even sellable with the other enchantment in it. Every day at noon, it releases any spells inside it all at once, hence the pinwheel of death."

"They made a damn bomb," I say.

Lawrence's eyebrows go up.

"Correct." Natalie thrusts her finger into the air. Her drawing fades out.

"Wait a sec…" I tilt my head. "How does magic know what time zone it's in? Would it still go off at noon in California?"

She sighs. "Noon is a simplification. The enchantment isn't really aware of time in the sense of what the clock's doing. It's sensitive to the energy flow between the Sun and the Earth relative to the position of the enchanted object on the surface. When the alignment of the cosmic radiation reaches a certain angle, the effect triggers. It's much simpler to say 'at noon.'"

"Right. Sorry I asked." I rub my forehead.

"So, someone committed arson with this crystal?" asks Natalie.

Lawrence grins. "Your friend is psychic, too?"

"No," says Natalie. "You're both wearing fire department uniforms asking about a device with a bunch of delayed release fire spells in it. I guessed." She waits a tick. "And you mentioned a restaurant being burned down before."

"So we did. Heh." He picks the crystal up. "Kinda lost myself in all this magic talk. Hmm. Brooklyn, you saw the back of a man's head, and we know this is the ignition source."

I reach for it. "Let me see that again?"

He hands it over. "Knock yourself out."

"Uhh, that might be more literal than you think." I look at Natalie. "How's this psychometry thing work?"

She raises an eyebrow. "You're asking the enchanter for help with psychic stuff?"

"An enchanter with a reading fetish." I poke her in the chest. "Come on, you can think of something, right?"

"Well. Okay. Gimme a sec." Natalie runs off into the back of her shop, humming. At the far end, she ducks past a purple curtain covered in silver stars.

Lawrence leans on the counter. He's calm, almost casual, and highly patient. I spend the few minutes while waiting for her to return gazing at the crystal and trying to read it like I can read people, but nothing happens.

"Here it is," singsongs Natalie, as she emerges from the curtain with a book. She leafs over pages on her way to the counter. "Okay, it says here, a clairvoyant will clear all thought out of their mind and try to think of nothing. Once they are able to center themselves, any latent impressions in the object should rise to the surface."

"Great. You know how difficult it is to think about nothing?" I ask.

She drops the book on the glass top, above a row of dark wooden wands. "Maybe you should try meditation?" Natalie folds her arms and rests her weight on the counter behind the book.

"Right. Clear my mind… Easier said than done."

They're both quiet, watching me ogle the crystal in my hands. I close my eyes and grip the little lavender gem in my right fist. Thinking about nothing gets me nowhere quick as my mind keeps leaping on random images. With that failing miserably, I try another approach: I think about the crystal and push the memory of the last image I got of it back to the tip of my brain.

Come on. Link. Open up.

Natalie's shop is so quiet, the sounds of us all breathing become distracting. Right when I'm about to give up and ask to take this little bastard crystal home with me, I feel a faint rip of energy, like something poked me in the forehead with a teeny knife.

Seizing on that, I envision forcing the slice wider and allowing energy in.

In a flash of green and sunlight, I find myself standing in a park. Or at least, it looks like a park. Lots of grass, trees, a somewhat-paved path lined with pushcarts and stalls. A carnival or something? One stands out: a woman under a blue-awning. She's behind a table in front of an old-timey wagon, like what snake-oil salesmen used to run around in with horses. This one's sky blue with white decoration, but no writing.

She looks sixty or so. I remember her dark grey hair from the first vision. She smiles at me as if she knows I'm watching, but that doesn't make any sense. It's got to be whoever bought the crystal she's reacting to. Who are you, lady?

The scene pulls away from me, sliding off into darkness. My eyes flutter open. Fortunately, I'm still standing. Didn't faint this time.

"Well?" asks Natalie. "You definitely did something."

"How can you tell?" I ask.

Lawrence is leaning back, both eyebrows up about as high as they can go. "Because your, umm, eyes lit up blue."

I put on a sheepish smile. "Is that normal for psychics?" I know it isn't. It's probably normal for whatever I am though.

"Dunno." Natalie opens the book again. "I'll check though. What did you see?"

"A park or something." I describe the vision, and the woman.

Natalie looks up from the book. "Oh, that sounds like Silverbough. It's a village about an hour west of here in the sticks. Lots of magey stuff and shops. Awesome, friendly people. I go there all the time."

"Guess that's our next stop," I say, giving Lawrence the eye.

8

SILVERBOUGH

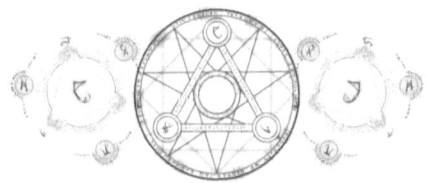

S ilverbough turns out to be a bit of a ride outside the city, but not too far west. Natalie explained the village has been around since colonial days, after European explorers chased the Native Americans away from a point where five ley lines intersect. This, of course, made it a magnet for those who use magic, those who aspire to use magic, and those who simply adore being around magic. Nowadays, the village is part one-stop-shop for magic users, part tourist-attraction, and part getaway/rest spa for practitioners.

The village got its name from the trees that grow around it. Take a wild guess why the trees got that name? Yeah. They're silver. Not metal, but the bark glimmers like it. White leaves, too. Nat had some pictures on her phone. So, yeah, we're driving toward the storybook woods.

Natalie visits it at least four times a year to buy supplies. Evidently, being an enchanter is a *lot* of work. Many of the reagents she needs have bizarre preparation requirements like 'left out in the light of a full moon undisturbed for one full lunar cycle' and stuff. Who has time for that? Not my friend. People invented magic before social lives existed, amirite? She makes enough money that she can pop over to the village that technology forgot and stock up on powders, oils, crystals, and whatever else she needs after someone else puts in the grunt work.

Guess that's commerce.

One nice thing about this temporary assignment, I didn't have to show up at the stationhouse at six this morning. Yours truly gets to work FMO hours until this investigation's over. Due in at nine and I still get to leave around six. It's a mini-vacation, except I'm probably going to have to be in next Monday, which is usually a day off. Ugh.

Lawrence is quiet on the ride, driving us according to the GPS. Neither one of us have ever been there, and I get the feeling he's not comfortable around magic, just like Hilleman, my new boss. I guess arson investigators like to deal with stuff they can themselves study up on and replicate, rather than rely on the word of so-called experts. Like me. That's fair, but boy, if he only knew what sat next to him. The thought puts a grin on my face. My gut (as opposed to my increasingly psychic brain) tells me of the fire department's arson team, he's the least freaked out in regards to magic, and probably the most laid back. Guess that's why he got stuck with me.

So far, I like him. He gives off granddad vibes, which is kinda cool. Gotta be my face. Must be that 'large eyes' thing. They make me look innocent. Fate *does* have a sense of irony, after all.

We pull off the highway a little after ten in the morning. A winding road leads us to a conventional small town, which we go straight past to more twists and bends among pine trees. Not long after the hamlet's gone behind a wall of leaves, the GPS leads us to the left at a fork onto dirt road.

Fortunately, we're in a department SUV and the path is no trouble for it. The occasional *clank* or *thump* of rocks hitting the wheel wells breaks the silence for a quarter mile or so before we round a sloping curve and a wall of silver greets us. It really is pretty. Looking at it makes me feel like I should be seeing elves cavorting around.

"Well, how 'bout that?" mutters Lawrence. "Damn, ain't that a sight."

I'm speechless.

The forest up ahead goes from normal to fantastic along a perfect line, like I'm staring at a colossal snow globe without a dome. Beyond the last row of normal pine trees, the woods look like nothing that ought to be on this planet.

Gnarled white trunks streaked with silver, like clusters of smaller trees braided together, create a canopy of glimmering silver leaves on wide-reaching branches. A carpet of rust brown, yellow, and dark red upon the ground conjures the feeling of an early-autumn day despite it being March still. Here and there, little balls of light, pastel blue, white, and yellow, glide about. I half-want to call them pixies as they dart and zip about like drunken moths.

"I think this is the spot," I say.

Lawrence resumes driving, following the road into the magical wilderness. I sit up straight and stare out at the trees, wondering if I'll see something strange like centaurs, unicorns, goblins, or the like. Alas, I spot nothing more bizarre than a couple streakers running around. The guy's got enough body hair not to need clothes. Judging by the flowers in the girl's hair, they're probably some combination of college students, vegans, hippies, potheads, or eco warriors.

The road brings us to an open area that's almost a parking lot. Two large, one-story buildings flank it, and a bunch of vendor tents take up the space between them except for a walkpath leading into the village. At a quick glance, they seem to be selling food, drinks, 'see the invisible' glasses, and funny hats. One's got a load of stuffed animals. Guess they get a lot of tourists.

"Looks like we're on foot from here," says Lawrence.

I stretch in the seat and a yawn crawls up from the depths of my soul. "Yeah. Unless they rent horses or something."

He finds a parking space, not difficult considering the lot's empty and there's no lines.

More locals emerge from the 'back rooms' of the booths to check us out. Must be the emergency vehicle and uniforms. A few even appear in the windows of the visitor's center on the right. Two guys in blue tunics and beat-up sandals push housekeeping carts around the other large building, a motel. Yes. Tunics. A pair of dudes dressed like medieval peasants are pushing plastic carts with mops, mini vacuums, and various cleaning supplies.

Oh, boy. I haven't had enough LSD to do this justice. I whistle and shake my head while shoving the SUV door shut. After a moment to soak in the surroundings—almost everyone is dressed like we've gone back in time—I take a few steps and meet Lawrence in front of our truck.

"Where to from here, boss?" I ask.

He chuckles. "This is your show, kid. I'm way out of my element."

"What *is* your element?" I grin. "Earth or Air?"

Lawrence shakes his head, smiling. "Neither. My element is a nice soft sofa and a cold beer."

"This is *magic* stuff." With a sigh, I start toward the walkpath leading in. "Evidently, I'm psychic. Not the same. I'm as clueless as you are."

He trots up beside me and slows to match my pace. "Aha, yes, but you are something. I'm plain ol' Lawrence Ellis. You're at least closer to this stuff."

Heh.

From the parking area, we walk up a mild hill to a flat courtyard at the end of a curve. A fountain at the center is alive with three statues: a nude elf woman, a male faun, and a dragon. The elf and faun are about waist high to an adult, and the dragon's on par with a brown bear for size. All are completely white, and probably made of stone, yet they walk around as if real. While the dragon 'breathes' water into the basin, the elf pours it from her vase, and the faun's flute projects streams whenever he 'plays.'

Dozens of vendor carts are scattered around as well as along three other paths leading deeper into the settlement. The central trail leads off to what I imagine is the village proper, full of oddly-shaped huts and homes, probably where the locals reside. Why anyone would want to live so far removed from technology, I can't even imagine.

A tortoiseshell calico cat gives me a strange stare.

"What?" I ask it.

The cat tears off into the weeds so fast tiny clods of grass fly off its feet.

Oops. Guess it sees my horns somehow.

That reminds me. I still need to talk to Mom.

I stop, stare at Lawrence, and concentrate on the image of the woman we're looking for, trying to push it into his head.

"You all right? Look like you're about ready to mess yourself." Lawrence chuckles. "You tryin' ta do something?"

Shit. I slouch, exhaling from the exertion. "Yeah. Trying to share the woman I saw with you. Guess you didn't see anything?"

"Only a bit of color in your face." He grins.

"Guess I'm a one-way radio then." I fold my arms and look around. There's still the old-fashioned way.

The closest vendor, a skinny thirty-something with long brown hair and a bushy mustache, stands behind a cart covered in penguins. Not actual penguins, mostly potato-sized figurines. A few outliers are two inches tall or the size of watermelons, but for the most part, they're about as big as a man's fist. He's got a black top hat on along with a wizard's robe, and brass-rimmed spectacles.

I approach. Oh, this is going to be weird.

"Hello and welcome to Malidore the Magnificent's Penguin Emporium! Can I interest you in a Spheniscidal companion? Or perhaps a war-penguin? Wait!"—he holds up a hand at me as if stopping traffic—"I know exactly what you're in need of." He picks up a squat, pudgy statue with a comically oversized beak. "This is my Magnum Opus."

"Your what?"

"Forty-four caliber." With a giant grin, he indicates two rather large nostril holes in the massive beak.

"Uhh, no thanks. I don't need any weaponized flightless waterfowl," I say. "We're here on official business with the Philadelphia Fire Department."

"Oh." He sets the 'gun-guin' down and indicates a ten-inch bird, which pivots its head to look at me. "Perhaps I could interest you in one of the Kings?" His eyes narrow with playful suspicion. "They're my bestsellers. Everyone hates cleaning their house, right? These little guys do all sorts of stuff. Pick up clothes, do laundry, clean the floors…"

"Interesting, but… one, I probably can't afford that, and two, I'm on duty right now."

Lawrence sidles up beside me, browsing the penguins. "They're kinda cute."

"Ahh, a connoisseur?" asks Malidore the Magnificent.

I'm shocked he didn't throw a 'the great' in there too.

"Heh, not rightly." Lawrence grins. "Magic an' me don't get along too well."

"Can you tell me where I might be able to find a woman who sells crystals? She's older, maybe sixty. Grey hair, shoulder long. Likes blue." I glance down at the king penguin statue. It waves at me. Oh boy. If Natalie's shop is any estimation, I can't even afford to look at these things, much less buy one.

"Oh, that sounds like Serena." The top-hatted vendor gestures at the left path leading away from the huge courtyard. "Little ways up that track there. Everyone needs a little penguin in their life. When you're ready, just come on back. I'll be here."

"Thanks." I flash a genuine smile.

Wow. Beyond merely selling them, the guy genuinely wants people to have penguins. I read it clear as day in his presence. I seriously need to find someone who can explain to me what I am and how I know this stuff out of nowhere. Hell, I might just stop by here one of these days, when I'm not on duty.

Following the penguin guy's directions, I lead the way out of the courtyard and head up the dirt trail. The locals continue to watch us with interest, evidently mistaking us for cops. Either that, or our modern clothes stand out.

At long last, a familiar sky-blue wagon comes into view on the left. The woman I've been seeing in flashes of psychic insight is behind a table full of crystals of every imaginable color or shape in shallow wooden trays. She glances our way and locks eyes with me. My 'read' on her is sparse, but tells me she's friendly with no particularly strong intention at the moment.

Her posture stiffens, but the kindly smile remains. Lawrence follows a quarter-step behind me on the left, content to let me do the talking. Like I'm any kind of authority on this stuff. Sigh. I should've brought Natalie along. I walk up to the wagon, as pleasant a smile as I'm capable of on my face. This adulting thing is hard. Being a surly teen took a lot less effort.

"Welcome to the Crystal Garden. I am Serena. What may I help you with?" asks the woman.

"Hi, I'm Brooklyn Amari, and this is Lawrence Ellis. We're with the Philadelphia Fire Department. I'd like to ask you a few questions, if that's okay?"

"Fire department, eh?" Amused at some hidden joke, Serena studies me for a moment before giving a curt nod. "All right, but I don't see how I could possibly be of any assistance to you."

I pull the crystal from my pocket and show it to her. "This was discovered at the scene of a recent fire. I'm evidently a bit psychic. When I touched it, I saw you. I believe this crystal came from your shop. We were hoping you could help us identify the man who purchased it."

Serena grasps my hand when I offer her the crystal. She pokes me in the palm with her left index finger and traces it across. The sensation sends a shiver down my back and into my leg. "Hmm. Interesting. You are not like most of your kind."

"My kind?" I raise an eyebrow before glancing at Lawrence. Crap. "Uhh, psychics?"

A knowing smile spreads over Serena's face. "That will do. Yes, among psychics. You do not give off... the same energy, if that makes sense." Again, she traces a symbol on my palm with her fingernail. It leaves no marks or glowing lights, or anything visual at all. "Perhaps it's your upbringing. I sense a great love from your... mother."

I stare at my hand in this old woman's grip. Despite being strong enough to lift and chuck a steel I-beam from a hotel, I stand there like a child trapped by their grandmother. "Yeah. Mom's great. She didn't deserve the life she got, but she's doing better now. Finally comfortable."

"You should come back and visit some time. I would very much welcome a chat." Serena winks and plucks the crystal up in two fingers. "Ahh yes, I remember this one. Dragon Quartz. Linzval."

"Linzval?" I tilt my head like a confused dog.

"His name." Serena raises her eyebrows. "I name all my babies."

I manage not to crack too much of a condescending grin, though my eyebrows furrow a little. "Right... Well, the man who got... Linzval from you enchanted it into a spellstore and loaded it up with fire. Used it as a bomb basically to burn a place down."

"Oh my." Serena's face reddens with anger. "That's reprehensible! I loathe it when people abuse innocent, beautiful things." She rubs her hand back and forth over it. "Oh, Linzval, forgive me for trusting that man."

Lawrence gives me the side eye. Yeah, he thinks the old one's a little off the deep end.

"I do remember the man who bought Linzval," says Serena. "He had a quiet sorrow to him. He asked about dragon quartz, and said he wanted a gift for his young daughter."

"Can you remember what he looked like?" asked Lawrence. "Did you get a name?"

"Oh, around forty, I suspect. Black hair with quite a bit of grey. Looks like he spends a lot of time in the sun. I want to say his name is Robert or Ronald or something." Serena takes a knee, and reaches under the table.

"Thank you." I face Lawrence. "Well, that only narrows it down to a few hundred thousand. Easy."

"One moment, young lady," says Serena. "I've got him on camera."

"Camera?" I ask, on the verge of laughing. "For real?"

Still on one knee, Serena points over her shoulder at a small black box on the side of her cart. "Magic isn't the answer to *everything*, you know. Sometimes, the mundanes can do things cheaper." She sticks her second arm under the table, and the clicking of computer keys starts up. "If you give me an email address, I'll send you the video file."

I draw a blank. Should I give her mine? Is there an official one?

Lawrence leans in and gives her his departmental email. Ooh, he's got a 'dot gov.' Hmm. Maybe I do too, but I don't often interact with the public unless I'm carrying them out of a burning house.

"Would you mind if I kept Linzval?" asks Serena. "He needs to be rather painstakingly purified."

"I think that can be arranged eventually, but for the time being, he's considered evidence. If we're thorough enough, there will be a criminal trial," says Lawrence.

"Oh." Serena lets out a sad sigh. "Of course. I hope you punish him for what he did to Linzval, though I don't think the man who bought this crystal is the one who enchanted it. That poor girl."

"Which poor girl?" I ask.

"The one whose present got stolen, of course." Serena blinks at me.

"Uhh, ma'am, I don't think there is a little girl. In my vision, I saw the same guy… black hair with a bunch of grey. He's the one who put the crystal in the place that burned. I'm pretty sure the daughter is a cover story."

"Oh." Serena folds her arms. "I suppose that's better. Any man who'd do that to a crystal would not make a good father."

Lawrence coughs to cover whatever noise he made at that.

Serena's anger fades to a mixture of curiosity and concern. "Now, is that it for the official business?" When I nod, she gives Lawrence a quick glance before leaning close and continuing in a quiet tone. "Let me know if I can be more of help. Oh, and do remember, if you need an ear, hon, you can always come back and talk. I've never met one quite such as you before."

Huh. Maybe. Gotta check in with Mom first. "Thanks, I'll keep that in mind. Might just take you up on the offer."

She smiles. "Farewell then. May your paths find favor."

Lawrence nods at her. "Thank you, ma'am."

An alarming thought circles my brain as we walk back down the trail to the village. Serena somehow knew what I am, or at least knew I'm more than I appear to be. How many others can tell that? Natalie's a mage, and she didn't notice. If not for that crystal of hers… Suppose it's one of those 'school' things. Whatever type of magic Serena possesses must let her see things.

"Once we get back, I'll run this video over to the PD. Let them see if they can figure out who this guy is. That's their job. Great work, so far," says Lawrence.

"Thanks." I wave at the penguin guy as we pass. It would be kinda neat not to have to pick crap up off my floor, but I don't have the time right now, and I think Nat might be offended if I bought some other enchanter's stuff. Then again, for all I know, she might find the penguins adorable. "So what now?"

Our official SUV chirps and unlocks as Lawrence hits the button on the fob. Once we're inside and the doors are closed, he pats me on the shoulder.

"You get off easy for now. I'll drop you at home. Stay near a phone though," says Lawrence.

"Never go anywhere without it." I gesture at my smartphone.

He starts the engine and backs around in a K-turn.

Great. An early day. Haven't had one of those since school ended. Yeah, this adult thing blows. I close my eyes, daydreaming about being fifteen.

9

A HELL OF A MESS

Relaxing was nice while it lasted. After a brief Wednesday, I got a call to 'go back to normal' for a while, so Thursday, I showed up at the stationhouse at six in the morning and endured the obligatory teasing about being 'one of the peons' again. No one seemed to care my 'promotion' to the marshal's office had been nonexistent—they teased me anyway. Oh well. Two days pass without anything burning, which is awesome.

Alas, hose drills suck.

At least it's Saturday and I'm not on rotation. I get to sleep in, and I'm going to drive up to Allentown to visit Mom.

Once I'm done sleeping in.

I drag myself out of bed a little past nine, which feels like I've slept all day, and go straight into the shower. Once I'm cleaned up, I throw on a black half-tee, non-frilly black miniskirt, and black leggings. Yeah. I like black.

Shoes can wait for now. In the kitchen, I stare at the fridge, trying to make up my mind between cooking an egg, having a bowl of cereal, or being überlazy and stopping at DD or Starbucks for breakfast.

"No!" The shout of the little girl next door comes through the wall so loud, it's like she's standing next to me.

Ugh. Now what?

Frank murmurs something too low to make out.

"I don't want to!" yells the kid. "Where's Mom? No! Let me go."

I don't like the tone in her voice. Forgetting food, I creep closer to the wall to listen better.

"It's okay, Ashley. You're a big girl," says Frank. "Big girls do this all the time. This'll be our little special secret."

"No! I don't wanna! Get off me! Mommy!"

A shrill scream follows.

Shit!

I bolt out into the hallway, pull a hard right, and skid to a stop in front of their door. It doesn't even occur to me that I'm barefoot at the moment; I rear back and stomp the door by the knob. In a flurry of splinters, the door whips aside and smacks into the wall with such force it sounds like a gunshot.

Frank's on the sofa, pretty much straight in front of me, facing to my left. Ashley's standing, trapped between his knees, squirming to get away from him as he's trying to pull her dress up over her head. The *crash* of the door against the wall almost gives him a heart attack, or so I surmise; he stares at me open-mouthed and sweaty.

Serena's voice repeats in my mind. *I loathe it when people abuse innocent, beautiful things.*

As soon as I lock eyes with him, such fury takes me that my horns and claws manifest. In that instant, his twisted intentions toward the child hit me full force. He wants her more than he wants Tracy, and he wouldn't have been gentle.

Neither will I.

Ashley takes advantage of his momentary paralysis. With a diminutive grunt, she wrenches away from his grip and pulls her dress down to cover her underpants. She spares me only a two-second glance before dashing into a back hallway, screaming for her mother, though she's clearly not home.

An inhumanly deep snarl seeps past my teeth. Every bit of the anger I'd felt when that man tried to lure me into his car thirteen years ago crashes over me all at once. I'm vaguely aware of Frank's scream as I charge. Leathery fluttering comes from behind me. Rage has pushed my shift all the way to armor plating. I dive, snatching him off the sofa like a giant hawk plucking a three-hundred-pound field mouse from a meadow.

We crash through the patio door amid a spray of glass fragments. I dive six stories down into an alley running behind the building, without a scrap of care if anyone's watching. My wings flare, billowing out and catching our fall. He lets out a gurgling cry as the landing hurts his leg; I barely notice the impact and drag him up again. At my transformed height, my hand around his throat holds his feet off the ground. He grabs at my wrist, struggling to pull away while my claws dig into his neck, drawing blood.

Frank's swollen, sweaty face glows blue in the light shining from my eyes. We're almost nose-to-nose, and his scent is nauseating enough to pierce into my awareness past my fury. He's succumbed to total panic at the sight of me and struggles against my hold, but he might as well be pinned under a car for all the good it does him. He seems to realize he can't throw me off, so he whimpers and begs, but his words are meaningless sounds.

Ashley's screams for her mother replay in my head. Snarling, I plunge my left hand into his gut up to the middle of my forearm and grab a handful. He gurgles and convulses seconds after my claws do their magic. I'm half-tempted to rip his manhood off, but I don't want to touch it. Besides, he wouldn't feel it at this point anyway. Staring into his eyes, I tighten my right hand until the rewarding *crunch* of vertebra emanates from his neck. His eyes loll back in his head.

After flinging him to the ground, I descend on him like a wood chipper. Overcome by disgust and anger, I rake my claws, grabbing and throwing handfuls of meat in random directions. When I come out of my blind wrath, I find myself crouching over a bloody mess. Most of the contents of his torso lay strewn around the alley, some bits stuck to the wall ten feet away. He looks like a pack of land-piranha got a hold of him.

Once I manage to calm down, my brain starts up again. Still breathing hard, I sit back on my heels and wipe blood off my face with my shoulder—the only part of my arm not covered in it. Shit. This is going to be difficult to explain. While I doubt the police would have much sympathy for Frank, they don't have much for vigilantes either... or whatever the hell I am on top of it.

I stare at the blood oozing between my fingers, dripping onto the pavement in front of my knees. No one's screaming or shouting. People around here have kinda become numb to street violence, but that usually entails gunshots, not bestial roars and splats.

Sorry, Mom. I think I'm going to have to postpone my visit.

10

WHERE SHE STANDS

I look around at the mess I've made, and eventually twist back to stare up at the sixth-floor balcony. Maybe they'll think he jumped as a suicide and exploded on impact? Calm, I shift back to normal. My shirt's missing, likely ripped apart by my wings bursting into existence. Tail's waving around too, but I think it only made a hole in the seat of my leggings. Skirt's fine. Great. I'm tits-out in an alley and covered in blood.

"He must've said something very inappropriate," says a deep-voiced man, with a hint of a chuckle.

I freeze, startled into paralysis.

A man who looks like he ought to be selling Mexican beer walks around in front of me. Expensive suit, salt-and-pepper hair combed back. Strong tan, a highly-sexy late-forties type. The most astounding thing about him though is his complete lack of reaction to Frank, or at least the collection of loosely-affiliated gore that used to be Frank.

"Umm."

The man tilts his head. "Don't worry about deception, Brooklyn. You can talk to me."

This is too weird. "So… are you like, the Devil or something?"

He laughs. "No. I am not. There is no such entity."

"How do you know who I am?"

The man tilts his head and looks me up and down like he's amused by the antics of a new puppy. "I have been watching you for many years."

"Only a *little* creepy." Creepier still is how I'm not getting any read of intention on him. It's like I'm staring at a mannequin without a mind. "You got a name at least?"

"I have many names. This particular human illusion, you can call… Dad."

What? I blink, staring dumbfounded for a moment. "You're my father?"

"Yes." He attempts a sympathetic expression.

"Bastard!" I roar, and lunge at him.

He makes no effort to avoid my fist, and I drive my knuckles straight into his face. 'Dad' sails about ten feet into the wall of the building across the street, cracking some cinder blocks.

"Not bad." He pulls himself out of the crater and rolls his shoulder while wiping dust off his sleeve. "You may feel I deserved that for not having been around, but I was held back by an arrangement."

I stomp toward him, winding up for another punch. "What you did to my mother, and you have the nerve to even try to talk to me?"

Dad leans to his left at the last possible instant, letting me punch my fist into the wall. Ouch. I think I broke at least two knuckles. Hurts like a bastard, but it's already repairing itself. Watching my mashed-up hand inflate back to normal distracts me from wanting to tear the head off the man who raped my mother.

"What is it you think I did to Reya?" He raises both eyebrows. "What did she tell you?"

"Nothing." I whirl on him, scowling. "She would never even talk about you. It's not hard to guess."

He shakes his head. "Oh, no. The particular activity we engaged in that resulted in your existence was a mutual situation. In fact, she sought me out."

"Bullshit." I spring at him again, this time with claws.

Dad catches my wrist, swings me around, and puts my back

against the wall. More cinder blocks crack on impact, but it didn't hurt... much. "I did not force myself on your mother. One might argue the situation was the reverse, but who am I to decline such a beautiful woman's request?"

"You expect me to believe that?" I scoff. "I... think I'm some kind of demon thing, which means you're probably a bigger demon thing, and demons always lie."

Dad lets his head sag, and emits a heavy sigh. "I wish I could've been around to give you some information sooner, but I was forced to keep my distance until you became aware of your nature."

"Forced?" I struggle to get off the wall, but the man's way strong. I've never felt so weak in my life. It's almost like I'm a normal twenty-something woman held by a pro wrestler. Not being able to overpower him is scary. I wind up hitting him with the big eyes without meaning to.

"If I let go, will you calm down and stop trying to tear me open?" asks dear old Dad with a smile. "At least hear me out."

I look down. "'Kay."

He releases my wrists and takes a step back. "Before I can really explain why you would have been killed if I showed myself to you before 'things happened naturally,' I must explain a little of what we are."

"Well, explain then." I fold my arms. "Wait, killed?"

"Give me a chance to get there. You use the term 'demon,' but that is something manufactured by humans. My kind are known as the Shaar'Nath. We have existed for many thousands of years, long before this realm ever came to be."

"Isn't that a funny word for demon? Wings, horns, tail? How wild I was growing up? Fuck's sake. I mean I just killed that piece of shit like I stepped on a bug."

Dad chuckles. "You did. Step on a bug, that is. The world won't mourn him. For reasons I am unaware of, your mother sought me out twenty-three years ago. Few humans are able to recognize us when we disguise ourselves, but she knew me."

I pace back and forth. "I'm having trouble believing that. Mom never wanted power. She barely even uses magic. She's not exactly what you could call a 'powerful' mage, and she's never once complained about that."

He sighs. I hate to admit it, but the deep timbre of his voice *is* somewhat soothing. "I never did understand her motivation that night. Please know that we are not 'demons.' We Shaar'Nath are beings from another plane of existence. Humans became aware of us a millennium or so ago, and created legends to explain what they did not understand. Don't have answers? Make shit up. Heaven, Hell, God, that Devil thing… all the products of fertile minds who filled in the blanks with creativity."

I laugh. Okay, that I can believe. "So we're not evil?"

"Our kind are given to violence, greed, anger, wrath, impulse, and hedonism."

"You just summed up my childhood in two seconds. Except for the greed part. I never really had that. Well, maybe. I did steal a PS2 when I was little. But it's not like I wanted to be rich."

Dad takes a step closer and puts his hand on my left shoulder. He's warm. Oh, eww. I thought of him as sexy when I first noticed him. Gah. "Are you all right?"

"Yeah. Bad thoughts." I shake my head and wipe my eyes to dispel any mixture of Dad and sexiness going on behind them.

He grins. "Now, the problem lies with the Elestari."

"Let me guess. They look like angels?"

"Humans have based their stories of angels on them, yes." He nods. "In their true form, they more closely resemble humans, though they are paler, taller, and have great, feathery wings. Our kind are adept with powers of the mind. Reading thoughts, knowing intent, abilities that humans refer to as 'psychic.' The Elestari are more akin to mages."

The super-hot bartender comes to mind. "Umm. I think I might've seen one. I couldn't read his intentions either, like yours. Does that not work on us?"

"It's more difficult to use those talents on our kind or Elestari. Humans are like books yearning to be cracked open."

Eww. I hope he doesn't mean that in a literal, bloody sense.

"Great, so are these Elestari things going to want to kill me?"

"Within the human kingdom, there exists an armistice. In fact, the very creation of the human realm is a physical manifestation of this truce." He puts his arm around my shoulders, which I find myself not objecting to. "For millennia, our kind fought a brutal war. Neither side had any advantage, though they kept grinding on."

"What were they fighting about?" I ask.

He shrugs. "I'm sure a reason existed when it started, but I am not that old. I suspect few remain in existence who truly understand, though it probably has something to do with the innate differences in our personalities."

"The Elestari are nauseatingly good and nice?" I cringe.

"Oh, if only." He winks. "Arrogant, sanctimonious, superior, insufferable... about the only good thing they have going for them is they're quite beautiful."

I roll my eyes. Great, maybe that bartender guy was going to tell me how worthless I am.

"After epochs of war, everyone knew that continuing as they had been would likely ensure the extinction of both groups. Still, neither side could simply stop fighting... so a delegation met at a point equidistant from the center of our respective realms, and they created the Armistice, or as you know it, the human world."

"So this is... a wall?"

"Of sorts, yes. I am talking about stepping across dimensional boundaries here, not a physical wall. The human realm acts as a barrier that prevents Shaar'Nath from entering the realm of the Elestari, and vice versa. Before this world came into being, our respective realms touched, and it was quite easy to travel between them. Now, we must enter the Armistice first and seek some way past it. It makes even one individual getting through difficult, and a large-scale force impossible."

"Oh. Well that works out. Stopped the war right?" I scratch my head. "So, why did they make humans?"

"We didn't." He leans back and laughs, startling a distant alley cat. "You must understand how long ago this happened. Shaar'Nath and

Elestari combined their energy into creating the Armistice. That magic included Life as well as all the elements. The process you learned about in school that the humans call 'evolution' did occur. Humans are the end result of many, many years of... I suppose you could picture it as having a fish tank that you neglected to maintain and all sorts of random things grew in it."

"Great, so we're tank mold."

That makes him laugh again. "Well, your friend back there might qualify, but no... Humans developed in our image, likely due to the essence of the magical energies that created this world. They resemble Elestari at their roughest, and our kind at their calmest. Those who can wield magic are closer to the Elestari. Those with mental gifts are more like us... With the exception that they are human, unlike you."

"I'm a half-demon, aren't I?" I look down at myself. "Is that why I'm this unnatural white?"

"Aside from your use of the crudism of 'demon,' that is essentially accurate." He pats me on the back. "Soon after your mother became pregnant with you, a collection of Elestari found me. They demanded I have no contact with or influence over you until such time as you realized on your own that you are not fully human."

"Weird. Wonder why. I thought angels are supposed to be all 'goody-goody.'"

"If you listened to the humans' description of 'angels,' which the Elestari are not, you would think so. They're self-absorbed as can be, and tend to regard humans like ants. Our kind treats the mortals better, but that isn't saying much. *We* do talk to them if they figure out how to ask, but we often ask for things in return."

I scrunch up my nose. "Huh. Okay. So, I'm not really a demon. Demons are a product of humans making up stories. I'm part creature from another dimension."

"That is correct."

"Is the Shaar'Nath realm full of fire?"

He grins, which I take as a yes. "Speaking of fire. There is much I can teach you now that I am able to."

Dad takes me by the hand and walks over to Frank. "Our kind

have a special relationship with fire. It surrounds us, a living manifestation of the energy inside us. Your kinship with flames comes from this bond, even though you are part human. Hold your hands out." He extends his arm, palm flat, in much the same pose I'd expect from a Pyromancer.

I raise both hands over the body.

"You shouldn't leave this here to be found." Dad taps me on the stomach, an inch above the navel. "This is your power center. Envision a great furnace within you. Whenever you peer into the flames, they see into you as well. The fire has life, as do you or I. Here, within the Armistice, it peeks in only under certain conditions."

"Flammable things."

"Correct. Do not feel guilt for putting them out." He smiles. "You only send it back where it belongs. Now. Draw upon the furnace inside you. Feel the energy rising up your core and traveling down your arms."

No, it's not weird that I'm standing here talking to my father about extraplanar creatures while he teaches me how to incinerate a guy I just ripped to shreds. Weird is me standing here topless, covered in blood, and having a casual conversation with my father.

I stare at Frank, tapping once again into my anger at what he almost did to Ashley. Warmth spreads over my abdomen. With Dad whispering guidance in my ear, I manage to light my hands on fire in about five minutes. It's kind of cute really in a dark, twisted way. Like a dad showing his daughter how to fish, only with more murder and concealing of evidence. After a bit of coaching, I pull off a double stream of flames from my outstretched arms that half-cremates Frank in seconds. For the first time in my life, fire has true heat.

"Whoa." I take a step back. "It's hot."

Dad beams at me, a proud father. "Excellent." He casually immolates the rest of Frank with one arm, guiding a shaft of dark red-orange fire around like a flamethrower. I stare at it, mesmerized, wondering if this is how humans feel around 'normal' flames. Once the bulk of the body is little more than a dark stain on the road, he creates a serpent of dark-crimson fire that races around in a graceful ballet, devouring all the globs I threw. When the last of the gore is ash, the fire-snake dissipates.

"That fire can hurt us, can't it?"

"No worse than a human sticking a foot in too-hot bathwater. It is significantly more potent than any fire that should exist here normally. The Elestari have no resistance, however they also have magic that affects us in particularly nasty ways."

I pinch the bridge of my nose. "Please tell me I'm not being dragged into some 10,000-year-old war."

"That's doubtful. The Armistice has existed for quite a long time." He flicks a tiny stream of fire at a piece of Frank sticking to the wall he'd missed, reducing it to a wisp of smoke. "I think we've forgotten about the war the same way we forgot how it started."

"So, what should I do?" I stare up at him. Holy crap. I have a dad.

"Be wary if you should ever encounter an Elestari. Other than that, you'll need to figure out where you stand in this world."

I look around. "What if I'm kinda happy with the way stuff is?"

"Then be happy." He pats me on the shoulder.

"Wow. Amazing no one noticed Frank. Thanks for helping me clean that up." I don't really do the hugging thing (except with Mom), so I wind up making a lame face at him.

"You're welcome." He winks. "It's not difficult to convince humans they don't want to walk down a certain alley or peer out certain windows."

Wow. That sounds like pretty powerful psychic stuff. "Can I do that?"

"Perhaps with enough practice."

Yeah. Hands on my hips, I look down. Oh shit. Right. Topless. That'll attract attention, and the coating of blood will cause problems. "I should, uhh, go clean up."

"That is a wise idea. We shall meet again soon." He grasps me by the shoulders and stares into my eyes. "Please know that I kept my distance only out of fear the Elestari would harm you."

How messed up is that? I'm part demon and angels threatened to murder me as a child if my father got anywhere near me. I guess they didn't want knowing what I was to affect me growing up or something. Bastards. Much better thinking Mom was raped? Gah. I'm really not liking angels these days. Wait. Not angels. That's mythology. I grumble. Sorting *this* out is going to take some time.

"How—?" I look up again, and he's gone. I lose a few seconds twisting left and right, searching the alley, but I'm alone with my tits. "Crap."

A scuffing sound makes me turn.

Ashley peeks at me from around the corner, face, and one leg visible. Her straight brown hair hangs down to her knee. Red rings her eyes, and she shivers, but she doesn't seem frightened. For a second, we stare at each other. The girl steps out into view, a wad of paper towels in her left hand, black cloth in her right. Her flip-flops drag as she tiptoes over to me and offers the clump of towels.

"I brought you a shirt from your 'partment. Your door's open," says the girl, her voice barely over a whisper.

I accept the gift and wipe the blood off my chest, somewhat. No sense putting on a shirt now since I'm covered in sticky. Still, I take it. "Thank you."

She breaks eye contact, looking down for a moment before sneaking a glance at the char mark. Ashley swallows hard, shudders once, and drags her gaze back up to meet mine. "You killed him."

"He's not going to hurt you."

Ashley flings herself into a hug and bursts into tears.

Shit. I've got 'child' on me. I grimace, not quite sure how to react to the situation.

One thing, I *do* know.

I need to get inside before someone sees me. Half-naked woman covered in blood with someone else's little girl? Yeah, that's going to take some explaining.

11

DARK ANGEL

Ashley's sobbing wanes to staccato sniffling breaths. She peers up at me and, with a look of total innocence, asks, "Do I have to unsummon you now?"

I hold back the laugh. "Gimme a sec, kid. I'm not wearing a shirt and I'm covered in blood. Need to go inside."

"But I brought your shirt." She tilts her head.

"It's going to take more than a couple paper towels to clean this. I don't want to ruin one of the few articles of clothing I have, especially after you picked it for me." I pat her on the head. "Thank you for the towels."

Hell with it. She's already seen me, and thinks I'm a demon.

"Come on." I pick her up, sprout wings, and carry her up six stories to the sliding door I smashed.

Ashley squeals, mostly from shock, but the sound coming out of her shifts to an almost cheer as we land. Ouch. Broken glass plus bare feet stings. I heel-walk into the living room. Thankfully, all the glass is outside on the balcony. After setting the girl down on her feet, I sit and pull tiny shards out of my soles. The fragments are already creeping up, forced away as my skin mends, so the process is quick and painful.

"Wow. Does that hurt?" Ashley squats nearby to stare at my bleeding foot as the wounds close.

"Yep. It hurts a lot. You shouldn't walk over broken glass without shoes on, 'kay?"

She looks up at me again. "Frank wanted to do something bad to me, didn't he?"

"Yep." I use the towels she brought me to wipe my feet before standing. No sense tracking blood around the carpet. "Don't ask what. I'm not going to explain it to you until you're older."

Ashley looks down. "I know. I saw Frank and Mommy together before. She said they were 'wrestling.'"

Ugh. This poor kid. Apparently, I'm still in my patrolling my trailer park from creeps in giant white cars mindset. "Where's your mom?"

"Work." She fidgets. "I tried to hide in my room, but he said he'd tell Mom I was bad if I didn't sit with him."

I take her hand. "Come on. I can't leave you alone." We head out the broken door (which *is* stuck in the wall) and go left to my apartment. Once we're inside, I close the door and lead her to the sofa. "Can you sit there and not break anything while I clean up?"

She nods and starts to settle in, but twists around to stare at me over the sofa back as I walk off. "Hey, wait. I'm the mage, and you're the summoned minion. Why are you telling me what to do?"

"I'm not a demon. I just kinda look like one."

Ashley gives me a suspicious squint.

"Are you scared of me?"

She shakes her head.

"There. You know I'm not a demon. If I was a demon, you'd be afraid of me because demons are evil, and little kids can feel that."

She blinks, unimpressed.

"Besides. A demon wouldn't have stopped Frank."

The child tilts her head at me.

"Right. Just sit there for a moment, please?"

Ashley twists back to face forward and flops out of sight. "'Kay."

I hurry another shower to get rid of the blood. So much crimson comes out of my hair, I keep looking up for a wiseass pouring blood on my head from a bottle. Eventually, I'm clean, dry, and dressed. I put on the black shirt she brought me with the same skirt as before, plus black-and-white striped leggings. Also, combat boots. Fuck glass. Ouch.

Ashley's still on the sofa where I left her. Amazing. But then again, it only took me about twelve minutes.

"Do you know your mother's number?" I pull out my phone.

"Yeah." She recites it.

I dial. It rings ten times and goes to voicemail. Second try, same result. The third time I call, Tracy answers after two rings.

"Who the hell is this, and where did you get my number?"

Everyone assumes some secret government agency is listening to cellular phone calls, so I play it vague. "Tracy?"

"Who the hell are you?"

"Nice to meet you too. Look, I live next door to you. Found your daughter alone. Your asshole boyfriend threw a chair or something out your patio door. Not sure where he is."

Tracy's quiet for a long few minutes. "Umm. Uhh. Is Ashley okay?"

"I guess you know there's a reason she might not be." I can't hide the venom in my voice.

"She's never liked him. I didn't want to leave him alone with her, but I didn't have a choice. Please, tell me he hasn't hit her?"

"Ashley's fine. You'll need to call the super about your front door. It's a bit damaged."

She coughs. "The front door, too? What happened?"

"No idea. Found the kid standing in the hallway." I wink at Ashley, who nods. "You're at work?"

"Yeah," says Tracy. "'Nother three hours. Look, I can get out."

It's almost noon. Couple hours won't be that bad. I can still make it to Mom's. "If it's gonna cost you money, I can keep an eye on her until you're done."

"Wow… uhh. I don't even know you, but… Thanks. Can I talk to her?" asks Tracy.

"Yeah. Sure." I hand the mobile to the kid and mutter, "I don't trust phones. We'll tell her what really happened when she's here."

Ashley nods and grabs the phone. "Hi, Mom."

She takes my paranoia to heart. The kid evades questions like a senator. Once she convinces her mother she's okay with me, she hands the phone back.

"I'll try to get out an hour early or so," says Tracy. "Thanks, I owe you."

"We'll talk when you're back."

Something in my tone makes her hesitate for a few seconds. "Okay."

Two and change hours pass. Mostly, we watch TV, and I order pizza for lunch. Poor kid eats half the pie. I revisit my opinion on wanting kids. Hanging out with them past a certain age, not so bad—as long as they're someone else's. I can deal with the babysitting thing. Diapers, tantrums, bedtime, sickness? Bleh. Not my job.

The doorbell rings at 2:49 p.m. Ashley's still laughing at the last joke I made about the purple cartoon gorilla on the screen, so I leave her to the show and get the door. It's Tracy. She's wearing a Starbucks shirt and black pants. Wow. Amazing she's making rent. Then again, this building's not exactly high end. Random shootings around here do wonders for making it affordable.

"Umm, hi," says Tracy.

I take a step back. "C'mon in. We need to talk."

She enters, craning her neck while looking around until she spots a bit of light brown hair poking over the top of the sofa back. "Thanks for watching her."

"Frank was attempting to rape her," I mutter.

Tracy starts to walk past me. "He just yells a lot."

I grab the woman by the arm. "You're not listening to me."

My strength shocks her blank-faced. She glances at my hand on her left bicep for a second before lifting her head to make eye contact. "He's not a bad guy. You just need to know how to handle him. He gets in his moods."

"He's not getting into any more moods. Your front door's busted because I kicked it in. He had her pinned between his knees. I caught him trying to rip her dress off."

She stares at me. "No... He's not like that. He's a little short tempered, but..."

"Tracy." I glare. My horns come out and I let my eyes change to glowing pools of energy that tint her blonde hair green, her pale face blue. "It's not angels who answer little kids' prayers."

Tracy about faints.

I go back to normal. "I'm kidding, but now that I have your attention." I explain again about barging in, and tell her exactly what happened to Frank. (Without the gory details.)

"Y-you're serious?" Tracy trembles. "He really...?"

"Yeah. The walls are thin. You need to start thinking more about that daughter of yours." Surprise radiates from her. She never imagined he'd try to attack Ashley like that, but she did expect some physical violence. "You left her there with him figuring you'd come home to what? Broken arm? Broken jaw?"

Tracy stares at the floor. "What am I supposed to do? I can't bring her to work. I can't leave her alone."

"You're her mother. You'll figure something out." I soften my tone. "Look, if you ever get stuck in a situation like that again, tell me. I'll send the bastard on his way."

She looks at me like a deer stranded in the middle of a six-lane highway.

Hey girl, you're the one who had a kid at eighteen or nineteen or whatever. Sure, I rolled those dice too (at sixteen) but got lucky and didn't wind up preggo. Guess I shouldn't hold it against her. But hell, if I'd had a kid? I think Mom would've exploded from disappointment... then peeled herself off the walls and taken care of both of us. Mom. Yeah. She's superhumanly patient.

"I suppose I can watch her if I'm here, but I work, too."

Tracy rubs her hands up and down her arms. "I guess I can figure something out. Uhh, thanks."

"Mom!" yells Ashley, finally noticing her here. She runs over and clings.

The woman sinks to her knees and breaks down crying, arms wrapped around her daughter. Ashley holds on, also sniffling, but looks happy.

"She saved me," says Ashley. "He was gonna 'wrestle' me, but Brook stopped him."

Tracy cringes, but can't stop crying.

"I'll… call the super for you." I wander over to the kitchen to give them some privacy.

ALL MY THREATS BOTH VEILED AND POINTY DIDN'T DO AS MUCH TO Tracy as when Ashley said she'd rather stay in my place than go home. I guess no mother wants to hear their kid say they don't feel safe around them and prefer the company of a total stranger. Fortunately, the kid didn't put up too much of an argument after I assured her that everyone makes mistakes, and this time, her mother learned from it.

Those two need some serious mother-daughter time.

As do I.

It is, admittedly, tempting to fly myself up to Allentown, but not during the day. At best, I wind up getting classified as a 'magical creature,' and have to register… which brings into question a lot of things like, would I be allowed to have a job at all, much less be part of the fire department? At worst, some religious wingnut thinks I'm really a demon and tries to kill me. I laugh at the idea of a wild-eyed hillbilly waving a cross at me as if it would do something.

Maybe I could claim to have a magical trinket that makes wings. That's not completely unheard of, but it's still hassle I don't need to deal with. So, a little after six, Saturday evening, I take a Lyft to a PEPTA station and drop twelve bucks on a portal service to Allentown. While stepping through a hole in reality is instant, I get stuck in a waiting area until there's 'enough customers' ready to go before the portal mage bothers to get off his ass.

I almost snicker at his outfit, a strange marriage of blue 'conductor's uniform' with wizard's robes. The hat like a little round cake is the perfect touch of ridiculous. As long as I live, I will never understand why some mages insist on the whole robes thing. It's 2017, for shit's sake. So what if they wore robes when magic was discovered? We used to murder each other with flintlocks and muskets, and they've been upgraded.

Sometimes, it's fun to think about what the world might've been like without magic. How would we travel long distances or create giant buildings? I suppose doctors would have to do more than treat minor injuries and sicknesses. The Lifemages can fix almost anything, but most are kinda full of themselves and don't want to be bothered for problems that aren't deadly, severe, or outside the ability of a mundane to handle. They're also rare enough that a society with as many people as we've produced couldn't effectively rely on them alone.

The mage approaches a rounded platform with three tiers, each about the height of a staircase step. He faces the waiting room, calls "Allentown," and turns toward the platform. While my fellow travelers grab bags and shuffle about to stand, he windmills his arms about and chants in a language I can't understand. Two tiny dots of glowing blue light rise up out of the topmost section of the platform, tracing lines in the air as they climb in the shape of an archway. The instant they touch, the space between them ripples like a soap bubble before melting away to a view inside the Allentown PEPTA station.

He continues muttering, one hand poised in a gesture reminiscent of Kung Fu. I guess he's holding it open or something.

I follow the group of about twenty into a mostly single-file line. Crossing the portal feels no different from stepping through a door into another room, though we aren't traveling that far. It must be strange to traverse great distances, walking out of heat into cold or the other way around. Ugh, it would take forever to get used to the time shift.

Anyway, once in Allentown, I hurry for the station doors, scurrying under a huge vaulted ceiling covered in moving paintings. This month, they've gone with a superhero theme. Last time I visited, it had a bunch of old-looking Renaissance style art. Made the station feel more like a cathedral than a public transit hub.

A long flight of stairs later, I'm at the curb, surrounded by food vendors and new arrivals waiting for taxis, friends, or whatever ride they've scrounged up. I do the same, and stand there people-watching for about fifteen minutes until an older guy with a white brush cut pulls up in a minivan. His face matches the portrait of the driver in my Uber app, so I hop in.

"Hey. I'm Andy. How are you doing?" he asks, smiling.

"Not bad." I fidget, trying to get comfortable in a back seat that smells like kids—a mixture of body scent no human can pick up, plus candy, soda, something fruity, and a touch of fart. Must be a boy.

Nothing in Andy's intentions sets me on edge, so I relax. Actually, he's giving off rather comforting vibes. Someone started a rumor awhile back about these private drive startups hiring nutjobs, but really, it's not like I've got to worry about a random perv.

Andy's already got Mom's address from the service, so he starts driving right away. He makes random small talk for a while, and I reply at an almost subconscious level, not really paying attention. Noise to fill the space.

"Ahh, spring break or something?" He grins.

I think that came right after I mentioned I was going to see my mother. "Thanks, but I'm not that young."

"Oh, sorry." He chuckles. "You kinda look it, plus no car. Assumed."

"Never got around to buying one. I don't usually leave Philly, and my job drives me wherever I need to go."

"No kidding. That's handy. Mind if I ask what you do?" White eyebrows tick up a notch in the rearview mirror.

"I'd ask what you do, but you're obviously an Uber driver." I wink. "I work for the city. Firefighter."

"No kidding." He blinks. "Wow. I'd never have guessed that."

Yeah of course not. No one does. I'm too 'pretty' or too 'delicate' or too 'female' to possibly be a firefighter, right? Female firefighters are all butch or something. Oh, and probably also lesbians. Since Andy didn't come off as condescending, I stifle my irritation and keep a pleasant expression.

"There's something about fire. Lost my house when I was a kid, and I guess I wanted to help others that sorta thing happened to."

He nods. "Nice. Nice. Better that than a cop. No one ever hates seeing firemen show up."

"Right." I glance out the side window at trees blurring by.

"Oh. Sorry. Firepeople? Didn't mean to, uhh, you know." He beats a drum solo on the steering wheel. Awkwardness wafts off him in sheets. "Duh. Firefighters."

"Something like that. Look, I'm not one of those women who gets bent out of shape over gender-charged words. Unless you're trying to say that only men belong slinging hose."

He slows for a red light and stops behind a flatbed truck full of logs. It makes him nervous for some reason. What, does he expect one to come flying at us and take his head off? "No, no, not at all. You don't look like the type of girl to do that sorta thing is all."

"What exactly do you expect 'that type of girl' to look like?" I ask, eyebrow up.

Andy laughs. "Ehh. Suppose I'm gonna stick my foot in my mouth if I answer that. I'll play it safe and say they would look 'older.'"

"Wise man." I grin.

We pull up to Mom's, a modest row house on West Allen Street. Scraps of Spanish conversation drift about. A pack of preteen boys plus two girls run around in the street chasing a soccer ball, shouting and cheering. Parents sit on porch steps or shake carpets out of windows. One woman yells at a dark brown boy around seven whose butt is half out of his shorts. The kid pulls them up, but they sag right away as soon as he sets off after the ball. It's not a lavish life, but it's a step up from the one I had as a kid. Then again, I miss the openness of the trailer park. This place feels too crowded.

The writing thing has been pretty good to Mom, though she's quite far from 'wealthy.' Compared to my childhood, however, she's rolling in money. Yeah, I ate a lot of bologna as a kid. Or rice and beans. Freezer waffles were big too. Wore the same dress all week long. Mom always said not having things makes you appreciate what you do have. I never faulted her for not being able to give me tons of clothes, toys, dolls, or whatever. Having to work such long hours and not being around as much as I'd have liked did piss me off, but I couldn't blame her for that. If she didn't bust her ass, we'd have been living in a cardboard box in some alley. Even with welfare, we barely made it.

I get out when the minivan door motors open. "Thanks for the ride."

"Have a good day, kid." Andy winks.

Once I'm out, he drives off in a cloud of dust, the automatic door closing on the way. I give him a ten-dollar tip (hey I'm not exactly rolling in it either) via the app and stuff my phone back in its holster.

A lot of curious looks come my way. I'm conspicuously white, more so than your average 'white person.' I've got my mother's features, but not color. She fits right in here. Her father's from Mexico and her mother was born in Puerto Rico. The fragrance of food in the air takes me back to my childhood.

Some other kids in my school got picked on for being Hispanic or African American, but they left me alone. At least until they saw me with my mother at a PTA meeting. Then I got teased for being adopted. I know I'm not. If you put me next to my mother in a black and white photo, no one would ever doubt we're related. I suppose I get my color from Dad's side of the family.

"Mama? Are you here?" I call out in Spanish while knocking. "It's me."

"Reya, your kid's here," shouts the old man next door before waving at me. He's perched on a metal folding chair next to a round metal table painted forest green. Three empty Budweiser cans stand by a fourth that, judging by the condensation, is about three-quarters full. His tank top is clean, but shows off his beer baby.

His front door is two feet away from Mom's; a flimsy little railing of wooden rungs separates the porches. Floral print shirts cover most of the railing on his side, draped there to dry.

"Hi, Hector." I wave. "How's life treating you?"

He makes a noncommittal noise while shrugging, and proceeds to complain about AARP, Medicaid, his two sons who never come visit, and so on.

Mom opens the door and pulls me into a hug. "Brooklyn! What happened? You said you'd be here around lunch time."

"It's a long story." I wave at Hector and let Mom drag me inside to the kitchen, where we sit at the table.

Her place is nice, though the décor makes it look more like an eighty-year-old retiree lives here than a forty-four-year-old self-published writer. Mom's got a thing for plates with artwork on them. They hang everywhere.

She gives me the worried smirk while lowering herself into a chair. "Are you eating?"

"Yes, Mom."

The usual barrage of questions goes by. No, I haven't found a boyfriend yet, but I have a date. Yes, I'm still living alone. Yes, still with the FD. No, I'm not going to get hurt at work. Yes, I know you want to be a grandmother someday. Ugh.

"Tell me what has made you so late," says Mom. "You are avoiding something."

I nod. "Yep."

She gives me 'the look.'

"I met Dad."

Mom stares at me for a long few seconds before glancing toward the stove. "I'm making pastelis."

Typical. Never talks about him. Okay, let's see if this gets her attention. I stand and pull off my t-shirt, exposing a racer-back sports top. This *is* still my mother. I came prepared.

"Mom?"

She looks up at me, a weak, hopeful smile that I'm going to drop the topic of Dad. Her expression blanks out when she sees me with my shirt off. "What are you doing?"

I unfurl my wings, knocking over a chair and swatting a colander off the countertop. The horns come out and I let my eyes glow. "I know why you don't want to talk about him, but I don't think it's the reason I'd assumed all these years."

"Oh, my God," mutters Mom. "I did everything they told me to do and…" She buries her face in her hands and sobs.

It's rather cramped in her kitchen, even without fourteen feet of wings. I shift back to normal and pull my shirt on before righting my chair and sitting. "What are you crying for?"

"You're… one of them still, but I did my best."

Hugging always makes me feel strange, except for Mom. Maybe whenever someone tries to hug me, I get pissed off that they're not her. As soon as I wrap my arms around her, she looks up.

"What am I? Dad had some ideas, but they sound crazy."

Mom wipes at her eyes and clings to me. "They warned me to guard you against the darkness. It was in your nature to be… evil, but you could fight it if I raised you properly."

"You didn't mess up, Mom." I hug her tight. "I'm not evil. Not even close." Killing isn't evil when it's bugs… or child molesters, right? "A little free-spirited, maybe."

She laughs.

"I mean it. Evil beings don't run into burning buildings trying to get people out. They pop open a beer, kick back, and laugh."

"Perhaps you are right." She takes a deep breath and sighs it out before gesturing at the stove. "Help me with dinner?"

"Sure. So, this 'they' you mentioned. Wouldn't happen to look like angels, would they?" I ask on my way to the counter.

Mom makes a clucking sound with her tongue. "You would think I've lost my mind and put me in one of those… homes."

"You're not even forty-five yet, Mom. You're nowhere near ready for a 'home.' And if you turn into one of those little old women who can't live alone, you're moving in with me. I've got wings, Mom. Why would I think you're crazy?"

"I don't want to be a burden. You have a life ahead of you. By the time I'm ready for Depends, you'd better be chasing some rugrats, or I might just move in with you like you ask."

I laugh while assembling pastelis. Mom always makes them in huge batches to freeze. My whole stationhouse could come over for dinner tonight and they'd all be stuffed. This ought to last her a few months. We chat on and off about random stuff: her neighbors, my job, the fire investigation, her writing. Once the pastelis are all put together and the rice and beans are cooking, I drag the conversation back home.

"Dad said there's no such thing as demons and angels." I give her the rundown. "I grew up thinking he... umm. Forced you."

"I don't remember why or how I found him." Mom stares into her lap while speaking in a weak voice. "I was unmarried. I'd never seen him before, but there we were, in bed. No..." She hesitates, air leaking from her throat for a second. This is *really* hard for her.

"It's okay, Mom. You don't have to explain if it's painful." I squeeze her hand.

She opens and closes her mouth a few times before her expression hardens, but she refuses to look at me. "He didn't force me to do anything. The memories I *do* have are so unlike me that I tried to think of it as a dream."

Yeah. Dad mentioned that she'd been the instigator. That *is* totally unlike her.

"When I learned you were on the way, I knew there must have been a reason for God to lead you into my life, so I decided to accept you with all my heart. Not once did I ever consider any option other than keeping my daughter." She finally looks up, making eye contact.

I continue holding her hand. The love she radiates is so powerful, and it makes me feel safe, just like when I was little and clinging to her after a nightmare. We share a quiet moment acknowledging what we feel for each other. For all the hell I put her through as a teen, she never once lost her composure and screamed at me. The worst she ever did was let the cops keep me overnight once. Okay, maybe more than once. Tracy had trouble finding a babysitter, and so did my mother. Cops got to look after me for a whole weekend when I was thirteen. If I remember right, a spray paint marathon at the mall put me there. Probably the most relaxing weekend of my mom's life during my teen years. She knew right where I was.

Fortunately, I didn't have a can on me when I got nabbed, and no one saw me do anything... but I got picked up for 'being with' the others.

Getting arrested (again) wasn't half as shitty as being forced to clean the walls. 'Course, I guess it beat doing six months in juvie. How could I say no to an offer like that?

Dad also mentioned the religion thing is made up, but I can't bring myself to pop Mom's bubble. It makes her feel better, and what's my opinion against thousands of years of people convincing themselves of something? I've often wondered how she could be a minor mage and still believe in that stuff, considering the various churches have been trying, by relatively similar means, to get their respective flocks to believe Lifemages are divine in origin. Never mind that the existence of even one person who wields life magic and doesn't believe in any gods or goddesses disproves the idea that the power originates from a higher being. Especially one who demands worship. Why would he, whoever he is, give power to someone who denies him?

And this just officially became a bit too heavy for my brain to handle right now.

"I hear you. I really am just trying to understand what the hell I am, pardon the pun... what did these 'angels' tell you?"

Mom shifts her gaze to the blue-flecked Formica between us. "If you had been raised by your father, you would become wicked and cruel, like the rest of your kind. They saw in me the ability to make a difference in you. If I raised you right, I could prevent you from falling into darkness, and make you human. The one who seemed to be in charge warned me that you would be a handful. Impulsive, brash, prone to seeking pleasure in the moment without thinking of the cost or effect it had on others."

She blushes hard, and I'm sure she's remembering that time she walked in on me about to have sex for the first time. It's embarrassing enough to ask Mom for sex advice, ten times worse when the two of us are in position right in front of her and I'm asking for tips. Gah, that boy almost threw up all over me from nerves, and it took her two days to look me in the eye again without going crimson-faced. In hindsight, I'm glad she caught us before we went too far.

"I have the best mother in the world. You turned a demon baby into a caring adult." I wink. "Well, semi-caring. Sorry for the wild ride."

She laughs.

"So, umm. Anything else? Dad said they threatened to kill me if he made contact with me before I discovered my true nature."

Mom gasps. "What? They told me they would protect me from him, that he'd try and take you away."

"They kept him away by threatening me. I suppose they were worried if he had any influence over me, I'd come out wrong, so they wanted to get rid of me when it was easy."

"Umm." She stands. "The rice is done."

"Okay. Maybe after dinner you can look into my stars."

Mom glances back over her shoulder. She's worried, but also curious. "All right. But you're going to eat first. You're too thin."

I grin. That's my mother.

12

THE ENDLESS WAR

On a whim, I call Jason the following morning, hoping this isn't his swing week. One week a month, we all cover both weekend days and get two other days off. Except for the guys who volunteer to always work the weekend. I prefer mine off, but it's not like I've got anything really to do with them, so I got a reputation for being willing to cover someone's rotation if they had something important to do, family stuff, mostly. Working six twelve-hour shifts in a week is exhausting, but we do have a fair amount of down time. Not like it's constant ass-busting.

I remain in my bedroom to minimize the banging going on at Tracy's. Workers showed up to repair the balcony door as well as the front door, and they're not at all happy about wasting their Sunday.

The phone rings a couple times before Jason picks up with a slightly cautious, "Hello?"

"Hey. It's me, Brooklyn. You busy tonight, and are you still up for a date?"

"Wow, yeah. No plans really except for the PlayStation."

I laugh. "What game?"

"*Grim Tidings,*" he says. "It's a fantasy set in a world without magic or dragons."

"Oh, sounds interesting. Is the storyline any good?"

We fall into an easy conversation about games that winds up with me telling him about how I saved my old PS2 like a beloved pet when my Mom's place burned down. He's as shocked I know my way around games as he is I called him, but it's a pleasant shock, and two hours later, my phone buzzes at me for a battery warning.

Wow. Holy shit, I'm a teenager again. Have I really been talking that long?

"My phone's about to die. Pick me up?"

"Later, or do you want to make a whole day of it?" he asks.

"We better get going soon. My mother expects grandchildren next month."

He coughs.

"Hah. Got you. I'm bored. Day sounds good."

"All right," he says over a chuckle. "See you in like an hour?"

I leave the phone charging and take my time in the shower, deciding to try some floral-scented body wash that's been sitting on the shelf for weeks—another impulse buy. Smelling like orchids isn't terribly necessary at the stationhouse. Figure I'll go somewhat easy on Jason and not dress like a gloom faerie for our first meeting. Still gotta have my black though. A t-shirt and jeans work, plus sneakers. Not like we're going to a fancy restaurant, especially around noon.

My phone rings once Jason's waiting out front. I head out into the hall and get a nasty look from a guy in white coveralls working on Tracy's door. When I return his glare, my read on him says he wants to go home. Okay, he's not pissed at me, just pissed in general. After rolling my eyes, I head for the stairs.

Jason must like being a firefighter, since he drives a red pickup. He even had a blue emergency light bar put on it. A grin forms on my face as I climb into the passenger seat. Never thought about that before. I can legally own a car with lights on it, even if they are blue. Maybe I *will* get something purely for the neato factor. Lieutenant Sims has been on my case about not having a car anyway, since I'm required to be available in emergencies. For some reason, the department didn't want to give me one.

"Hey." Jason smiles.

"Hey yourself."

"So, I was thinking we spend the afternoon at Fairmount Park?"

"Never been there." I shrug. "Sure, why not."

We spend a few hours wandering the park and talking. It's quiet here. Reminds me of back home before I grew up. Philly's great, and I've got no sudden desire to leave, but I wouldn't necessarily mind being back out in the sticks.

Jason and I might share a fondness for video games, but our musical interests are pretty much polar opposites. I'm into metal, goth, and punk, and he's all about 90's pop. Ugh. At least he hates boy bands. He doesn't talk too much about his past, which gets me thinking it wasn't something to write home about. Or write home in general, once you've made it out of there. When we wind up at the Shofuso House, standing on a tiny bridge watching Koi, I fire an experimental salvo.

"Visited my mom yesterday. She's obsessed with grandkids, I didn't joke about that." I shake my head. "I'm not in any hurry, though. Are your parents on you about it, too?"

He fidgets, clearly wishing this little bridge had railings to lean on, and winds up putting his hands in his pockets. "Ehh, I don't really talk to them much. Never got along with my dad, and my mother was rarely around."

"Sorry." I feel a glimmer of anger and violence come over him for a second, but it's more a memory than a desire. His old man must've hit him a lot. "Forget I mentioned it."

He forces a smile. "Not your fault."

"Still, I made you think about it." I step off the bridge onto a little grass-covered island in the middle of a giant pond.

Jason walks up behind me and wraps his arms around my middle. "I think about it anyway. Hmm. I love the way your hair smells." He leans closer, sniffing at the back of my head.

I giggle. Whoa. Where'd that come from? I don't do 'cute.' I don't think I've giggled since I was five. "Orchid Rain. I'm not really into the frilly stuff, but sometimes I get strange impulses."

"I'm usually Mr. Play It Safe. Something about you pulled me out of my comfort zone. I had to ask you out."

"You had a little help." I turn in his arms to face him. "I did kind of push you. Still feel the same way?"

A genuine smile shows his teeth. "Yeah."

"Doesn't bother you who my father is?"

He tilts his head. "Should it?"

Sensing his confusion, I make a little flapping-wings gesture. "You know…"

"Oh." He laughs. "That."

"Yeah, that," I say with a grin. "My extra bits don't bother you?"

Jason shakes his head. "Nope. I don't really understand why, either. You'd think they would."

"Yeah, you'd think." I lean against him. "It's nice having someone I don't have to hide from."

"Secret's safe with me." He leans closer, eyes half-closed.

Oh what the hell. I kiss him. I can tell he's new at this. Probably even a virgin. Bonus. I get to corrupt another one. We've been officially on a date for about three hours, and there've been a few guys in my past where we'd wound up in bed in less time. Of course, in those cases, both of us expected nothing other than a brief moment of pleasure. Jason's entirely different. I find my lack of impulse simultaneously bizarre and intriguing. Or maybe it *is* an impulse—not to cheapen this.

Surrounded by a massive koi pond and trees, we hold each other and kiss for a while until a couple with two small kids, a boy and a girl, cross the bridge. The father gives Jason a disdainful look.

Ugh. Seriously? I am *so* sick of being mistaken for underage.

Huh. I wonder. I'm half-human. How long do Shaar'Nath live? Maybe I still technically *am* a teenager. My impulse control is weak, but much better than it had been when I lived at home. I even manage to get to work on time without the 'screw it, I'll find a new job' that happened a few times when I didn't want to roll out of bed. Good thing summer work for seventeen-year-olds with perky boobs and big eyes came easy. Made some decent money waiting tables that year, and I didn't mind the later hours.

Judgmental-Dad wanders to the edge of the island, still evil-eyeing Jason over his shoulder. A small telekinetic nudge to his foot makes him trip over himself and go face-first into the lake. Oops. There's that poor impulse control again.

His kids laugh while his wife screams… until she realizes the water's only thigh deep.

Our romantic island crowded, we leave and wander all the way across the park to the Mann Center, but they're doing some sleepy theater thing instead of a band. Jason whips out his phone to check on something, and after a moment or two, smiles up at me.

"Wanna grab dinner? There's some open seats left at Maxwell's. It's like a dinner-theater thing. Stand-up comics tonight."

"Sounds great." I wrap myself around Jason's arm. "Let's go."

IT'S NOT EASY TO HAVE A CONVERSATION OVER A MEAL WHILE A PARADE of up-and-coming comedians are doing their routine on stage nearby. Some are okay, some are on the bland side, and one guy was so horrifyingly lame that the switch on his microphone kept turning itself off. When he tried to brace the switch with his thumb, I telekinetically yanked the wire out the end. Gotta give him a little credit though. He changed up his act into a self-deprecating routine about his jokes sucking so bad even the ghosts hated them.

We make plans to hang out at my place for a little while and see how compatible we are with video games. Maybe we'll do more, but I'll let him lead for now. For once, I'm willing to wait and see what happens.

The show ends a minute or three after 10:00 p.m. Parking in this section of Philly is a pain. We walk the three blocks back to where Jason's pickup truck is, only to find a little Honda Civic stuffed so far up his back bumper, it's probably violating sodomy laws. The Lexus in front of him is less than an inch away.

"Shit," mutters Jason. "Asshole." He scowls at the Civic. "That's not even a full space. The idiot's double parked."

"That's not what double parked means." I stand by the passenger door. "If he parked here, that would be double parked. Two lanes."

"Still. How the hell am I supposed to get out?" He groans. "Guess I call the police or something."

I saunter over behind the Civic, since there's not enough room to get between it and Jason's truck. "Wait. I think I can get this."

He stares at me for a second before looking around. At this hour, there aren't *too* many people out and about. I stoop and grab the back bumper of the little Honda. No sense being subtle since Jason already knows my secret.

"Anyone watching?" I ask.

"Hang on." Four seconds later, he says, "Clear."

The Civic's a lot lighter than I expected. It doesn't take much straining for me to lift the rear end off the ground, edge to my right, and drag the little POS onto the sidewalk. I face it toward the street before telekinetically floating it sideways so it's wedged with the nose at a telephone post and the back bumper against a hair salon. Let the guy explain *that* to the cops.

"Holy shit," says Jason.

I dust off my hands, again giving the area a quick scan for dumbfounded eyewitnesses. I'd prefer not being tabloid fodder if I can help it. One thing about a big city. The locals tend not to see anything that doesn't directly concern them. Case in point. No one's reacting to my idiot-relocation project.

No one, at least, except for the almost seven-foot tall guy with model looks and straight blond hair, who's walking straight toward me.

Shit.

"Uhh, let's get going," I say over my shoulder, while staring at the bartender from Niflheim.

The too-perfect man fires a stare at Jason, who seems to freeze in terror. Something supernatural happened, but I have no idea what. That gets my hackles up, so I step in front of Jason defensively. Mr.

Perfect strolls right up, close enough to reach with a fist, but merely stares down at me.

"I tire of these games," says Mr. Perfect.

I narrow my eyes. "Got a problem with me moonlighting as a meter maid?"

"Your deception is as thin as your blood."

"What's your fuckin' problem, man?" I lean toward him, itching to hit him.

He frowns. "Clearly, you are."

"Oh, wait." I raise a finger and close my eyes as if thinking real hard. "I've heard about you. Only an Elestari could be such a sanctimonious fuckstick."

He sneers. "Uncivilized wretch. I have yet to figure out what your plan is, but I know you have been stalking me, and I intend to see to it that your machinations fail." With that, he gracefully sweeps his right arm out to the side and a glimmering gold-and-silver broadsword appears out of thin air, surrounded by a wisp of golden light. The blade has a mirror finish with hairline engravings, while the golden hilt is stylized like feathery wings. At the pommel, a silver pyramid holds a glowing ruby as big as a grape.

The sight of it makes me forget about being pissed. "Wow, that's like pretty and shit. So cool."

"What game are you playing at?" He leans his nose higher, evidently not expecting the genuineness in my awe.

"Probably something we can co-op like *Special Operations: Panama*. Oh. Wait. You're not talking about PlayStation, are you?"

"Quite not." He glowers.

"You know of all the guys I've met, I've never had one show me his sword so fast. Then again, I've never seen one so big."

"Crude." He grumbles. "You surely are your sire's offspring."

Oh yeah, I'm pissed at this guy. Screw the pretty sword. "Look, shithead. I'm not stalking you. We went to Niflheim *once*."

He raises the blade, pointing it at me.

It's astoundingly pretty, but I don't like having it waved in my face.

I take a step back. "You're overreacting, man. There's no plan. I'm not up to anything but trying to be on a date."

He narrows his eyes. "Your kind are known for deception."

"You're an Elestari, aren't you? If you're supposed to be the 'good guys,' why are you threatening an unarmed girl?"

"Oh, spare me." He lowers the blade to his side. "You're far from helpless."

I stare into his glimmering emerald eyes. If I was totally superficial, I'd be all over him. This guy could be in movies. But I don't care how pretty a guy is if he's such an arrogant prig... "Slow it down a bit, bud. I only found out about this whole Shaar'Nath thing a couple days ago. It happened on its own when Jason was about to die. I had to drag half a building off him and carry him out of a blazing inferno. Where were you guys, huh? Aren't the 'angels' the ones who're supposed to be helping humans?" I smack myself in the forehead. "Oh, that's right, humans are ants."

At the word 'angels,' he scowls harder. "The humans are misguided."

"So are you." I jab a finger at him. "The only scheme I'm up to is to go home and relax for a couple hours before bed, and then I get to go back to work *helping* people. I don't give a shit about any interdimensional war, Armistice, or how long your fancy sword is. The *only* reason there's a problem right now is because you're in my face."

"Hmm." The Nordic god gives me a long, condescending stare. Eventually, his sword dissipates in a glowing whorl of golden mist. "There is something different about you. If you are involved in some greater plan, I'm almost ready to accept that perhaps you are truly unaware of it."

I edge closer, as 'up in his shit' as a five-foot-six girl can get on such a titan. "I don't know much about any war, and honestly, I don't care. I'm no demon. I don't consider myself evil. Okay, so I killed two guys, but they both were the worst kind of scum."

He scoffs. "As if I would care what you do to humans? They're little more than moss growing on the bricks of the wall protecting us from your kind. You will not be permitted to threaten the Armistice."

"Permitted?" I lean in more, my tits touching his chest. "Why would I *want* to threaten this Armistice thing? My father said some rather not-nice things about your kind, and I see you're desperate to prove him right. I like the world just the way it is."

"Hmm." He turns away. "That has yet to be seen. For the sake of your continued existence, see that your opinion does not change."

When he walks off, I flip open the wallet I pickpocketed when my hips touched his thigh. Hmm. According to his license, he lives in Philly.

Daniel clears his throat.

I look up. He's standing over me again with his hand out.

"Since I'm being stalked, I wanted to know who was doing the stalking, Daniel Graf." I place the wallet in his hand.

After a silent smirk, he walks away again.

"Asshole," I mutter.

When I turn back to Jason, both he—and his truck—are gone.

Son of a bitch. I turn, feeling alone in the middle of nowhere. How the hell am I getting home?

Guess I could always wing it.

13

ROSSELLINI'S BISTRO

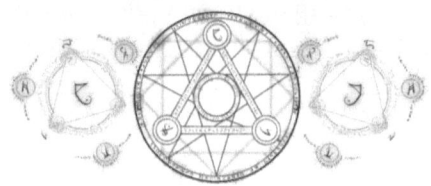

Monday morning, I get a call from Lawrence asking me to meet him at the department's arson lab. Some cases get farmed out to third-party companies, but after a private lab in Florida getting caught tampering with results cast a shadow of doubt over a thousand convictions, the brass has become distrustful of outside contractors.

I try calling Jason a few times, but he doesn't answer his phone. Half of me is hurt/pissed off, but I'm also fairly sure Daniel Graf (he of the big sword) did something to him. Question is… what.

My neighbors have been quiet, save for the occasional din of a television. Ashley doesn't strike me as a yeller. When she was over, her voice didn't get much past a whisper the whole time. Her mother has a set of lungs on her, but without the catalyst of an asshole, she doesn't react. Silence is such a nice change. The next time Natalie is over, we'll be able to watch a movie in peace.

Lawrence's call interrupted me checking out car dealerships online. Car services are going to get expensive if I have to keep going to random places. I don't need anything too big, but with my job, I also can't use 'the roads are snowy' as an excuse to stay home. Since I am still sans-car, I catch an Uber to the arson lab. My uniform keeps the driver quiet, though he's probably itching to ask me why I'm not using an official vehicle.

On the ride, the radio personality comments about a certain small car found in an impossible parking space, and throws around a few theories as to how it wound up that way. The sidekick suggests a mischievous imp. I'm not sure those are real. Then again, aren't imps a form of demon? I grin the rest of the way to the lab.

The front desk people don't recognize me, and I wind up stuck there arguing with them for a little while until I call Lawrence on my cell. When he emerges from a back hallway and confirms I belong here, the two guys apologize and admit they thought I was an academy hatchling trying to work a dare.

Sigh.

He leads me down a corridor with plain white walls, shiny white linoleum, and life-draining fluorescent lights.

"Lawrence, do I really look like a kid? Are my eyes that big?"

He makes a show of looking me over before grinning. "To me, everyone who hasn't hit forty yet is a kid. You've got a youngness to you, yeah, but you ain't no down-covered chick."

"Thanks. So, any news on our guy yet?"

"Not a damn thing." He grumbles. "Cops are lookin' for him, but they haven't come up with anything more than a name yet."

"So, why'd you ask me to come in today?" I try not to sound annoyed at him interrupting my day off.

He swipes an ID card at a reader and pushes open a heavy door, also painted white. "I'd like you to take a look at something else if you don't mind."

"Sure, why not. I'm already here."

The room beyond is dim and full of shelves bearing cardboard boxes labeled with dates and place names. He heads down the middle row and plucks a box labeled *Jul 2016 – Port Richmond* from the shelf, which he carries to the far end of the room.

A steel table stands along the back wall with three folding chairs tucked under it. Lawrence sets the box on the table, opens the lid, and removes a plastic bag containing a partially-melted wind up miniature grandfather clock about as big as a stick of butter.

"This was ruled an 'arcane device,'" says Lawrence. He's hesitating —and concerned.

"The other investigator, the one Hilleman wouldn't talk about, he was working on this?"

"Yeah. He jumped off a building after lighting himself on fire." Lawrence bows his head, the grey in his afro glowing from the overhead lights. "The whole thing stank. Sam was a solid guy. They ruled it suicide-by-insanity, but the only way I think he'd have done that, jumped, is to make the burning stop."

I stare at the model clock. "You think someone else lit him on fire, and rather than die an agonizing death, he wanted it fast."

"*If* he jumped, it'd been on account o' someone else lighting him on fire. Though I ain't convinced he wasn't pushed." He gestures at the bag in my hand. "And I want to nail the guy who did it to him. Figured I'd ask you for help. Plus, the firebug who did it is still out there."

"All right." I sit in one of the folding chairs, set the bag down, and open it. "Least I can do for your friend, but no guarantees."

He drags another chair out a bit and lowers himself with a grunt. "Understood. Thank you for trying."

"Okay to touch it?" I ask.

"Yeah. Cops have tried to fingerprint it already, nothing."

I stick my hand in the bag, hesitate for a second, and grab it.

A wave of glee passes over me along with visions of a tiny screwdriver tightening miniature screws and tweezers adding gears to spindles. I'm sure whoever made this was even more over the top with loving their craft than Serena. That woman treated her crystals like her children; this guy's a hair's breadth from having sex with his device.

The vision shifts to the clock standing on a doily-covered table. Hands tick closer and closer to the witching hour. I brace for something, but midnight strikes with no effect. I focus in on the second hand creeping onward. At midnight-plus-thirty-seconds, something inside the clock flashes bright red, the only spot of color in an otherwise black-and-white vision. Flames burst forth and fill the room.

With a jolt, I'm outside the building, hiding in an alley, watching flames fill the windows of a row-house. A great sense of gratification comes on, getting stronger when voices inside start screaming in terror and pain. The mood takes a disgusting turn that makes even Frank seem closer to human.

The revulsion knocks me out of the vision. I shiver in the chair with a hand on my gut as I try not to throw up all over the evidence room.

"That bad, huh?" asks Lawrence. When I only look at him, he gets up and rubs my back. "You okay, kid?"

I shudder. "That man is disgusting."

"Can you talk about it?"

"Yeah, as soon as I convince my breakfast to stay down."

"Oof," says Lawrence.

A moment or two later, all the foreign emotions are gone and I no longer have to fight to keep ownership of my fried eggs and toast. "The same man made that as set the fire. He got off on it, on the screaming."

"Sick bastard," mutters Lawrence.

"No… I mean"—I pantomime a guy stroking it—"he literally got off when the victims inside started screaming. Hearing them die in agony aroused him."

Lawrence shakes his head, his expression somber. "I wish I could say I'd never heard of that before. Some pyromaniacs have a fixation from early childhood trauma. Could be his mother beating him, maybe he got abused. Somehow, he formed an association between fire and pleasure."

"More like burning people alive and pleasure." I swallow bile and cough. "How many died there?"

"Eight. It spread over multiple houses. The fatalities all occurred in the origin building plus the two closest. Everyone else had time to get out. Some firebugs like to watch their work, and it sounds like that's what you saw."

"Yeah." I cringe. "You already checked dashcams from the police cruisers, I bet, and didn't get him. He was hidden in a tiny gap between buildings across the street."

"All the lights and activity out there, damn unlikely anyone spotted him in the dark. Don't suppose you got a name or a look at him?"

I rake my fingers through my hair and shake my head. "No. But I think I'd recognize his, umm, feel on another object. Have there been any other fires started by a device like this?"

"Only your crystal at Rossolini's Bistro."

"And that's not the same guy." I let out a long exhale. "Not even close. The crystal had little emotion from the guy who planted it, and I didn't even see it being enchanted."

Lawrence nods. "Someone merely doing a job."

"Yeah." I gesture at the clock. "*This* guy loved what he did."

"How would you feel about a permanent transfer to AI?"

I shrug. "I dunno. It feels like it's my calling to run into places and try to help people. I mean, I guess this is still helping, but less direct. I'll think about it."

He raises both eyebrows. "It's a pay raise."

"Okay." I smile. "I'll think *harder* about it."

WE TAKE THE FIRE MARSHAL'S OFFICE SUV TO THE SCENE OF THE restaurant fire. The property's covered with beat cops keeping sightseers away from the ruin. A bald almost-fifty guy with a horseshoe of black hair around the back of his head and a navy windbreaker climbs over debris, taking pictures.

"Insurance investigator." Lawrence points him out with his eyes. "They can help sometimes, notice stuff our guys miss."

I open the door. "He's here looking for any excuse he can find so his employer can refuse to pay out. They're not trying to catch bad guys."

Lawrence grins and shuts off the engine. "When we get lucky, the two align."

The cops greet us, all smiles, and we wind up BS-ing with them for a few minutes.

"You guys find anything yet?" asks a short, but muscular officer. Her nametag reads E. Rivera.

"Working on it." Lawrence nods toward the ruins. "Going to do another walkabout. Just to be thorough."

Rivera's partner, a white dude who looks like he's been back from the Marine Corps for all of eight hours, laughs. "Gotta be a case of 'restaurant isn't doing well, burn it for insurance money.'"

I glance at his nametag. Officer Hunt might have a point. The guy who planted the crystal sure felt like he'd been doing a job. "Kinda what I'm thinking too."

"Word is," says Rivera, "The dude who owns this place is chummy with the Mob."

"Maybe they used it as a front to smuggle griffon down, or Starshell?" asks Hunt.

Lawrence shakes his head. "Doubtful. If there'd been any Starshell in there, everyone within two blocks would've been seeing vapor trails and talking to interdimensional gods when the place went up in smoke."

"That only happens if there's an arcane ignition source." Hunt pauses, closes his mouth, then cringes. "Oops. Forget I said that. Not out in the open yet, is it?"

"You guys are fine." Lawrence grins. "Don't say that to the media yet though."

"So who owns it?" I ask.

"Fella by the name of Michael Rossellini. Real smooth one, that." Rivera hooks her thumbs in her belt. "I hear he's not too deep in, but he's got friends. Couple of detectives stopped by earlier. Got the feeling they're thinking it's organized, too." She adds in Spanish, "Ain't no one gonna go down for this."

"We're working on it," I reply in kind.

She gives me a shocked look and cracks up. We chat for a little bit about my mom and where I grew up. Yeah, the human half of me is

Mexican/Puerto Rican, but... that snow-white thing throws people off.

Lawrence takes a step toward the former building. "Starting to feel like this is getting complicated."

"You sound disappointed." I give the cops a 'take it easy' nod and follow him over to the wall.

"Ehh, you do this long enough, you get cynical sometimes. Mob involvement on a restaurant fire, no one died or even got hurt... little interest from the brass, less interest in throwing a bunch of resources trying to pin charges on a guy made out of Teflon."

"Slippery, huh? All that means is we need a sharper tack. Gotta at least try. Next time, someone might get hurt." I hop over the wall.

"Ahh, kids." Lawrence grins at me. "Ever optimistic."

I spend a while traipsing around the burned-out restaurant, picking up random things that catch my eye. Forks, a couple spoons, candleholder, other burned bits of appliances I can't even recognize anymore. Nothing sets off any visions until I'm in the area that used to be the kitchen, and I find a serrated, pointy knife with a bent tip. The imprint isn't so strong that it forces its way into my head on contact, but I can feel something there.

A little concentration opens the psychic door, and I'm treated to a vision of three guys standing around a wooden table. One, a handsome guy in an expensive suit, is holding the knife and waving it around while shouting. He's disappointed, and furious at an older man across the table. The grey-haired guy's got his hands clasped in front of him, and a severe disapproving frown on his face.

Surging with fury, the man with the knife rams it point-down into the table, shouting, "Goddammit!"

Reality fades back. The imprint is brief, and forged in anger. That's interesting. I carry the knife back to where Lawrence is waiting. He'd decided not to get ash and gunk all over his shoes since he has no psychic gifts. I relate what I saw.

"Got a picture of this Michael Rossellini?"

"Not with me, but..." Lawrence takes out his phone and summons Google. A few finger-taps later, he holds his phone up so I can see a man, late thirties/early forties with slick black hair, dark tan complexion, and brown eyes. He looks like the ambitious son of the don in half the Mafia movies ever made. You'd think if the guy really had connections to organized crime, he wouldn't wear the costume.

"Yeah, that's the guy."

Lawrence slides his phone back in its holster, grinning. "Sounds like either his Mob friends or dear old dad told him to pull the plug and he didn't really want to."

"Maybe the guy liked having a restaurant." I start toward the SUV. "Why don't we go ask him?"

ON THE RIDE TO ROSSELLINI'S HOME, I STARE INTO SPACE, THINKING about my father. He told me the Shaar'Nath are all what humans refer to as psychic, with 'mentalist' type abilities, which makes me wonder if I can do more than lift 'impressions' from people. Normal humans have occasionally claimed to be able to read minds or see into dreams.

I shift in the seat and face Lawrence, fixating on his eyes while slowing my breathing and attempting to see into his head. He glances briefly at me before returning his attention to the road. Minutes pass as I form and rearrange intention within my head, trying to find a way to 'push' mental energy to open the doors of his brain. It might be easier if I knew for a fact it would work. All I have is hope.

"You're either about to soil your pants or something's really bothering you," says Lawrence.

I close my eyes and exhale to give my brain a rest. "Trying out a new trick. Not sure if it will work, though. I've never done anything like it before."

"What's that? Trying to see my future? I'll tell you if you want to know. Florida. A beach. A drink in my hand that's either a margarita or some bright fluorescent nonsense." He grins for a moment before sighing. "Still like ten years out though."

Again, I focus on his eyes, and my desire to know what's going on behind them.

... bastard light is gonna turn red on me. Yep. There it goes.

"Whoa."

We stop at the light and he looks over. "Whoa? I stopped in time."

I grin, shaking with excitement. "I got it to work. I heard you think. Called the light a bastard."

The deep brown of his face gets a bit grey. "Uhh. That's a little unsettling."

"Sorry. I didn't get far in. Only like the tip of your brain." I face forward, head swimming.

I managed to read his thoughts, immediate as they might've been, far from deep into his mind... and that made me tired. New muscle, so to speak. Going to take getting used to. Heck. Do I *want* to be able to peek at everyone's thoughts? Some people remain friends only because they can't read each other's minds. Of course, in that situation, I suppose the truth of 'friends' is debatable.

"When we get there, I'm going to try that on him." I grin with eagerness. "Even if I can't dive all the way into his head, if you ask him questions, the answers might float across where I can see."

"All right, but I don't think it'll stand up in court. This ain't magic, and there ain't enough psychics out there for 'em to have made laws about warrantless mind reading."

I frown. "Yeah, but maybe it'll point us in the right direction so we find something the police *can* use."

He nods.

We're quiet for the rest of the ride, about six minutes. Michael's got a nice house in Bala Cynwyd. Fair bit of land, pool, two stories—probably five or six bedrooms.

"Guess there's money in burning restaurants down."

Lawrence laughs. "This would be his first. We already checked on that. No pattern."

I hop out and lead the way to the front door. Once Lawrence catches up, I ring the bell.

Michael Rossellini answers in person, though I'm not sure why that surprises me. He looks strange in a t-shirt and boxers, but his hair is still perfect. "Can I help you? Oh, is this about the bistro?"

As in the truck, I focus every scrap of my intention on Michael's eyes, trying to invade his mental cloud.

"Sorry to bother you at home, Mr. Rossellini," says Lawrence. "I'm Lieutenant Ellis from the Arson Investigation unit. We're following up on a lead on a man by the name of Ronald Harris. We believe he's the one who started the fire."

Shit. How did they find Harris? Michael keeps a perfectly straight face. "Harris? I don't know anyone by that name. Are you sure it wasn't some random crazy, or an electrical problem?"

"The man who tipped us off claims to have seen you meeting with him," says Lawrence.

Those backstabbing motherfuckers. I catch a flash of a tavern chasing the thought, a scrap of a green sign with the word 'Otto's.'

"Someone's playing you, lieutenant." Michael's expression is perfect detachment.

"A witness claimed he saw the two of you meeting at a bar called Otto's," I say. I don't have the finesse to talk and peek at the same time yet (maybe that's not even possible).

"I'm afraid to tell you that someone's wasting your time." Michael smiles. "I don't frequent 'bars,' Miss. When I drink, it's either at home among friends or at *nice* restaurants."

What's James up to? I did everything they wanted.

"So you have no idea where we may find this Mr. Harris?" asks Lawrence.

He thinks of an older, potbellied guy in a green shirt behind a bar. Maybe he didn't meet Harris in person, but a guy who subcontracted. I think we need to go to Otto's.

"Not a clue. I'm telling you, I never met the guy." Michael shifts his weight, losing patience.

"Thank you, Mr. Rossellini. Sorry about your restaurant. I heard you were quite fond of it." I offer a mostly-believable smile.

There it is. A twang of regret. He really did like the place.

"I appreciate that. Maybe I'll try again someday." Michael backs into his house and closes the door.

When we're halfway across the front yard, I mutter, "Someone forced him to burn it. He didn't want to. I almost feel sorry for the guy."

"Heh. Not sure what good any of that did." Lawrence beeps the SUV unlocked.

"Know a place named Otto's? I think we should talk to the bartender."

OTTO'S TURNS OUT TO BE A WORKING-CLASS WATERING HOLE NEAR Fitler Square. It's early in the day yet, barely one in the afternoon, but there's already a handful of old guys working on their second or third pints. It smells like leather and furniture polish, with an undertone of deep fryer oil. It sits on the corner, and feels bigger on the inside than it looked outside. Eagles pennants and jerseys cover half the room, while the other's a veritable shrine to the Phillies. Two dartboards in the back have different logos, one a Steelers icon, the other the New York Giants.

The guy behind the bar is the same guy I saw flicker by in Michael's head. He carries his weight weird. Except for his belly, he's got a thin frame. Looks like he's smuggling a golden retriever under his sweater.

I walk up to the bar near him.

"Hey, little lady. Got ID?" asks the man.

"Thanks for the compliment, but I'm not here to drink." I gesture at my assistant arson investigator badge. "I'm looking for a guy by the name of Ronald Harris. We heard you put him in touch with Michael Rossellini."

The bartender grins at me like I told a good joke. I manage to get my focus up in time to catch a scrap of thought. *That ain't even his name. This chick has no clue.* "Name don't ring a bell."

"Hmm. That's rather curious," I say. "When the police pull Mr. Rossellini's phone records, I'm sure they won't find a single call connecting him to your tavern."

This little pixie don't know what she's messin' with. "It would be unlikely, seein' as how I never called no Mickey Rosso-whatever." *Who's a rat?* His thoughts leap around over dozens of people who've hired him to 'make problems go away.'

My eyes widen. This guy usually sends men his thoughts call 'cleaners.' Eavesdropping on his head seems to get easier when I *don't* look at him. Instead of trying to see what's rattling around between his ears with my eyes, I find myself sensing where his cloud of consciousness exists, and delving into it by mental 'feel.' Arson isn't usually his game, but he knew a guy. A phone number floats into my awareness.

Impulsively, I grab a napkin and a pen from the bar and jot it down.

As soon as he sees it, the bartender slaps his hand on mine, pinning the napkin, trying to pry it away from me. He's pissed, but also flustered.

Lawrence lunges for the guy and gets two fistfuls of his shirt collar. "Get off her."

I grab the bartender's wrist with my free hand and squeeze. "It's all right, Lawrence. I got this."

The bartender looks back and forth between us, breaking out in a sweat.

"You sure?" Lawrence glances at me.

"Yeah." I lean forward, nose to nose with the bartender, and shift my eyes into their Shaar'Nath form: glowing pools of blue light. After a second to let the man's brain grind on that, I make them normal again and whisper, "Someone owes me a soul, and if I can't find him, you're next on the list."

"Gah!" yells the bartender. He releases the napkin and mutters, "Guy's got an apartment in Harrowgate somewhere. I dunno the address."

"Thanks." I give him a sweet smile. "Hope I don't need to come back."

Lawrence gives me a 'what the hell just happened' stare, but follows me out to the SUV.

Once we get in, he stares at me for a while. "Did I see some kinda blue light?"

"Yeah, you did."

"Was that some kinda psychic shit?"

"Yeah, it is." Technically, maybe?

He slides the key in the ignition, shaking his head. "Anything more you need to tell me?"

Maybe I should. Especially if we're going to be working together. Assuming I want to be transferred. Feels like a waste for me to not stay a front-line firefighter and take advantage of being immune to flames. Of course, a transfer might not prevent me from volunteering to gear up and go in. Meh. Not yet. I still haven't sorted out how *I* feel about all this. I hold the napkin up in two fingers. "Yeah. I got a phone number."

14

PROFESSIONAL ANONYMITY

Lawrence has a couple friends in the police department who are able to turn the phone number I got into an address, which isn't publicly listed. They lifted the name Martin Bradstreet from the system. Also, we learned the cops are still working their way through a bunch of Ronald Harrises within a reasonable radius of Philadelphia. I'm convinced that's a fake name at this point. It's common enough to be generic without sounding like John Smith.

Apologies to anyone actually named John Smith.

Guys with that name probably like being asked 'is that really your name' about as much as I like being mistaken for a seventeen-year-old.

A little after two thirty (we stopped for lunch), Lawrence pulls into the parking lot of a six-story apartment building. The C-shaped structure 'hugs' the parking lot on three sides. No fire escapes on the inside face, only a bunch of balconies with metal basket-type railings. Ugh. If this place ever burns, it's going to be a pain in the ass to deal with. I'm almost glad it's out of our district, though we still might get pulled in if it's bad enough.

We park and go inside, up to the second floor. The apartment we're looking for is near the end on the left wing. Our knocking and doorbell ringing gets no response. Either our guy's at work (not likely), out burning something else down (improbable so soon), or there's something else going on (I'm betting on that).

I rear back to punt the door in, but Lawrence waves me off.

"Ease down there, Amari. We're not cops, and as far as I know, this place isn't on fire."

Easy enough to fix. I glance at my hand. Kidding. Seriously. I'm not going to burn down homes so we can search a place. "So…"

"Let's see what we can find out from the super," says Lawrence.

I follow him back to the middle of the main wing and down the elevator to the first floor leasing office. At least it's close to the lobby. A bored looking woman in her late forties sends us to the basement office in search of 'George.'

The stairs down are also conveniently close to the lobby, and sure enough, a door labeled *Super* is in eyesight from the bottom. Lawrence knocks, and I do my best to stand with authority so I don't look like some intern tagging along. Grr.

A man inside yells, "T'aint locked."

What ought to be a living room is set up like a workshop. To the left as we walk in, a skinny sixty-something with John Denver hair and thick glasses stands behind a wood-paneled counter covered in papers, some of which are probably from 1962. He pushes his glasses up by the knot of white tape between the lenses and squints at us. Breathing in here tastes like I'm licking the inside of an ancient oil-burning furnace.

"Howdy," says George. "You two just move in? Don't reckon I've seen ya 'fore."

"Pleasure meeting you." Lawrence extends a hand. "I'm Lieutenant Ellis with the Philadelphia Fire Marshal's Office, arson investigation unit."

"Aw, shit." George rummages at the massive pile of paperwork. "Sorry. Got so much crap here, I'm sure I forgot to file them certificates."

"We're not here about certificates," I say. "We're looking to speak to one of the tenants. He isn't answering his door, and we're concerned."

"Oh." The old guy pushes his glasses up again, and smiles. "Not here about the certificates?"

Lawrence shakes his head. "No. We were hoping to check on a tenant of yours."

"Is there any way you could let us take a look around in there? It's related to an ongoing arson investigation."

"Oh, sure. Anything for you guys. My grandson's with a volunteer brigade over in Ardmore." George walks out from behind the counter. I half-expect to see an enormous wad of keys, but he's only carrying a white plastic card.

How 'bout that? Guess this building is more modern than it looks.

Lawrence gives me a 'careful' look, which gets me to peek at his head. *We ain't cops. This is thin ice. If there's anything in there, we could get it tossed by going in without a warrant.*

I nod. "Yeah. If we find something, we back out and you get one of your detective friends on the phone."

"This ain't no television show," says Lawrence as we follow George to the elevator. "Warrants don't come down that fast unless there's like a missing kid in imminent danger, and in those cases, no one waits for warrants anyway."

"Well, we'll wing it." I wink. This time, I don't mean that literally.

When we reach Martin Bradstreet's apartment, George whips out his master keycard and swipes the door open.

"Someone pays the rent on this unit, but far as I can tell, ain't almost never anyone there. Fine by me. Less wear and tear on the property. Y'all go on and do what ya need ta do. I'll be downstairs if y'all need anything."

Lawrence stands there radiating unease while George walks off. I shrug and push the door open.

"Wow," I say, my voice bouncing off the bare walls.

The place has an Ikea sofa, a small throw rug, a coffee-table-on-wheels, and little else. I wander in, looking around. Lawrence's shoes click on the hardwood, echoing. In the kitchen, I find a tiny table and two chairs that probably came with the place. Martin's got nothing in his fridge but a box of baking soda.

"No one lives here," says Lawrence. "Bet the guy keeps the apartment as a place to meet."

I close the fridge and start into the hallway toward the bedroom. "You're probably right. Fridge's empty."

"We're out of our league."

At the bathroom, I peer in. It smells like dust. "How do you figure that?"

Lawrence appears at the archway between hall and kitchen. "Organized crime? Arsonists and assassins managed by a guy pretending to be a bartender? This is the sort of crap the FBI ought to be dealing with."

"I don't think we're going to need that warrant. This place looks empty. Bet the bed's never even been used." I nose into an immaculate bedroom that also smells like dust. A quick glance around reveals nothing of interest, but a strange feeling comes over me, like the way I can tell when the stereo is on but playing silence. "Hang on. Something's off."

"What?" Lawrence walks up to the door, but doesn't enter the bedroom.

I cross the room to the window, sparing only a brief glance down at the road. The feeling gets stronger as I round the foot of the bed, and weakens when I go left toward the nightstand. Backing up makes it stronger, and the sensation leads me to the closet.

"There's something in there I can sense."

He moves over to stand beside me. "Any idea what?"

I put my hand on the door. "No. I've never felt this before. I told you I don't have a lot of experience with magic stuff."

"You're going to open it, aren't you?" he asks.

"Yep." I grab the knob and yank the door aside, revealing a plain closet with a single man's suit hanging within. I start to frown, but a trace of light on the back wall catches my eye, so I push the suit out of the way to the right.

Someone drew a sigil on the wall at eye level. A dagger-blade element points downward, with a snake curled around the upper part. Two triangular shapes at the top point off to the sides, giving the mark the overall appearance of the letter T.

"Nothin' there," says Lawrence. "'Cept a cheap suit."

"Do you see that?" I point at the sigil.

"The wall?"

"You don't see the glowing mark?"

He shakes his head. "Nope. There's a mark there?"

"Yeah." I snap a picture of it with my phone, but the mark doesn't register. A miniscule smear shows up where it is, an imperfection of the picture that I wouldn't have noticed if I hadn't seen the mark. "It's got to be magic."

"Why are you seeing it and I'm not?"

I can't help myself. "I'm psychic."

He laughs. "I walked into that one, didn't I?"

"Yeah, just a little." I wonder...

As soon as my fingertip touches the sigil, the back wall becomes an opening into a forest. At first, I think it's a super high-definition screen and someone is messing with me, but a cool breeze laced with hyacinth blows in.

"How 'bout that?" Lawrence scratches behind his ear. "A damn private portal. Where's this go, ya figure?"

"One way to find out."

"Not sure that's a good idea." He puts a hand on my shoulder. "Don't trust portals."

I look at him. "You never use the PEPTA? They don't feel like anything."

"No, ma'am. I drive." He smiles. "Don't trust magic."

"All right. Wait here then. I'll be right back." I step through.

"Aww hell." He closes his eyes and jumps, landing on the soft dirt behind me with a *thump*. "Is everything still where it ought ta be?"

"Yeah." I turn in place, looking around. The portal hangs like a towel on a clothesline behind us, between a pair of trees the same width apart as the closet. A matching blue sigil adorns one, which reassures me we won't be trapped if it closes. "Now *this*, I wasn't expecting."

15

A HOUSE IN THE WOODS

I advance, still looking around at the trees.

"We're in the Coventry Woods Preserve, 'bout fifty or so miles west and a bit north."

"Wow," I say. "You got that from looking at trees?"

Lawrence laughs. "No, from my GPS app."

His phone screen shows a massive blot of green south of Douglassville, with a pin damn near in the center. We've got at least a full mile of dense woods in every direction, much more than that to our west. At least we're not *stuck* here. The portal is two-way.

"So why on Earth would someone make a portal out here to the middle of nowhere?" I ask.

"For him, it's not the middle of nowhere."

Good point.

"Sec." I head over to a tree and sneak my claws out. Pulling myself up is pretty easy considering I can drag a Honda Civic around. I weigh a bit less than a car. From my new vantage point, I spot a squarish house fairly close by, due west from the portal. It's got two stories, a giant skylight, a deck, and a pool. Wow. Our guy's living nice, even if he is so far from civilization, he could set off an

Implosion Crystal and no one would notice. Fortunately, no one's invoked one of those things since Nagasaki.

It's *so* tempting to glide down, but I haven't let Lawrence in on that yet, plus I'd have to take the department polo off. Can't really do that while clinging to a tree trunk. So, down I climb. Lawrence braces my hips when I get low enough to reach in case I fall. Aww. That's nice of him. Fortunately, his gentlemanly approach keeps his eyes away from my claws until I can put them away.

"Anything?" he asks.

"Yeah. House. Over here." I point and start walking.

There's no trail or any obvious sign of frequent travel, but I *think* I'm going the right way. A few minutes later, Lawrence shouts from a ways behind.

"Brooklyn? Where'd you go?"

"I'm here!" I yell.

He steps into view out, over a hundred yards back. White polo shirts are pretty easy to spot in a forest.

"Lawrence!" I wave.

He turns toward me but doesn't react and keeps going.

Grr.

I trot back to him. "Hey."

He emerges from the trees. "Oh, there you are."

"You're not that old." I wink. "It's this way."

Again, I stride off toward the house, but within a minute, his rustling diverts off to the side.

"Lawrence. You're going the wrong way."

He stops, turning in place. "I lost you again. One second you were there, and the next, you disappeared."

"Stand still." I walk over to him. When I'm about six paces away, he jumps back and yelps.

"Gah! Don't do that to an old man."

I narrow my eyes. "I didn't do anything."

He points. "You appeared out of thin air."

"Oh." I biff myself in the forehead. "There's a ward on this area.

Somehow, I can see through it, but it's fooling you and making you walk in random directions."

"Once more in English?"

I take his hand. "I think the guy who lives here is a mage. He's put magic around his house that makes most people subconsciously walk around his property without realizing they're avoiding it. For whatever reason, it's not working on me."

"Oh." He fidgets like a frightened boy. "Did I mention I don't like magic? Nothin' against mages, you understand. I wouldn't much like anyone jugglin' lit Molotov cocktails either."

"That's fair," I say. "Come on."

"Wait a minute. This could be a mage, and the guy who burned the place. We're not cops."

I keep going, tugging him along. "If that's true and this guy's a Pyromancer, I wouldn't be too worried."

"Aww, dammit. You kids think you're untouchable."

"I've got more going on than I look like." I stop and glance up at him. "If you want to wait out here, that's fine."

He gives me a frown of resigned acceptance. "I'm not letting you go in there alone. We have no idea what to expect. We're out in the middle of nowhere. If he thinks we're a threat to him, no one will find our smoking bodies."

"If he does anything worse than talk to us, he'll regret it. He's going to know someone used his portal and disappear. By the time the police show up, this whole house could be gone."

He hangs his head for a few seconds, but winds up nodding. I take his hand, and walk him over the ward.

Once I'm sure we've passed the perimeter of the enchantment, I let him loose and trot off. The thrum of a pool filter breaks the silence soon after, and the trees give way to a clearing around the house. There's no garage, and no car in the gravel driveway. I'm pretty sure he either created this house out of thin air or moved it from some suburb. Short of a dirt bike or an ATV, no motorized vehicle is coming anywhere near this place, at least not without a shitload of trees being cut down.

Being ballsy usually puts people off guard, so I stroll right up to the front porch and knock.

A man in his thirties with neat, light brown hair and green eyes opens the door a moment later. His pink button-down and khaki pants are the furthest thing from what I expected to see. He looks at us, baffled, an expression that's probably mirrored on my face. A Girl Scout cookie line comes to mind, but I'm supposed to be professional, so I swallow it.

"Can I help you?" he asks.

"Are you Ronald Harris?"

He tilts his head. "No. And you are?"

Lawrence introduces himself. "We discovered an enchanted object responsible for a fire, and the trail leads us here."

The man in the pink shirt flashes a smug smile that makes me fight the urge to punch it. "Tell me, Lieutenant Ellis, if an individual purchases a firearm legally, and then uses said firearm to commit a crime, do you often harass the man who owns the gun store? I may or may not have enchanted an object, but I can no more control what my customers do with things than a proprietor of a weapons store."

"The object in question was enchanted to release a bunch of spells all at once. It makes no sense to do that because it's a useless spellstore. You had to know the person planned to use it as a weapon," I say.

"What else does anyone use guns for, dear?" asks the mage.

"Bombs are not guns." I make an explosion gesture. "What you made is legally considered a 'destructive device.'"

Lawrence fidgets at his pockets. "I'm not entirely familiar with how the law handles issues of a magical nature, but if your comparison holds water, then you would not be held criminally liable for what was done with your product. However, if you fail to assist us in locating the individual responsible, you may be committing obstruction."

Ronald Harris is not long for this world. The man's eyes harden. *This is why I do not work for cretins. My privacy is paramount. These two have overstayed their welcome.* "I am not at liberty to discuss who seeks my services. Confidentiality is one of the reasons my clients do business with me. And as I am sure you know, betraying certain organized individuals is bad for my health."

This guy's itch to dismiss us like peons lights a fuse in my temper. I loom at him. "You know what else is bad for your health? Pissing me off. Where's Harris?"

"Whoa, Amari." Lawrence grasps my arm. "Calm down."

I know he means well, but his patronizing tone only irks my inner demon more, powering a blast of mental energy that leaves the mage blinking and disoriented. Information floods into my awareness.

"So, you're Craig Eaves?" I turn toward Lawrence. "He's afraid someone named Ernesto is going to kill him. Who's Ernesto?"

Eaves gawks at me in shock for a second before flinging his right arm up. A serpent of flame lances outward from his fingertip and strikes me between the breasts, vaporizing a five-inch hole in my shirt and melting my bra, which snaps around behind my back under my shirt. Damn, that's annoying! The flame is awkward-hot, like initial groin-to-water contact when lowering myself into a fresh bath.

I glance down at the hole, and sigh. "You really shouldn't have done that."

The mage tilts his head, his arm still pointing at me.

Lawrence's eyes practically bug out of his skull. His head does a little side-side wag between the woods and me. He clearly wants to run before another firebolt has his name on it, but doesn't want to leave me.

Aww. He's so sweet.

I snarl and take a step closer to Eaves. "I'm going to try that one more time before it'll take a Necromancer to get any information out of you. Who. Is. Ernesto?"

16

RESISTING ARREST

E aves stares at the hole in my shirt. My boobs are nice, but I wouldn't go so far as to call them 'shock and awe' nice. He's trying to wrap his brain around the lack of burn.

"I'm getting impatient," I say.

He darts back into the house. Figuring he's either going for a bigger weapon to kill us with, or another portal to escape through, I chase. Lawrence yells something I don't catch. Eaves jumps over a couch in the lavish living room and grabs the doorjamb on the other side to take a hard right turn into a corridor without falling over. I leap the sofa as well, and tear after him.

The mage reaches the end a few strides before me and slams a door in my face. I don't slow down, ramming my shoulder into it hard enough to pop it clear off its hinges and send it flying into a large room with a skylight ceiling two stories up. The slab of wood bounces off a crude life-sized statue approximating a human figure, and crashes to the floor.

Eaves rushes around behind a desk near the back wall, which is mostly window with a sliding glass door that looks out over the pool area. Two long tables, made of the same light-stained wood as the walls and ceiling, run along both walls to my right and left, full of mage paraphernalia. Bottles, scrolls, candles, the kind of strange glassware I haven't seen since chemistry class, and jars of powders.

"What's the matter, Craig?" I growl. "Are you involved a bit more than a gun store owner?"

He points at me and says, *"Drazh."*

The statue tilts its head forward and its eyes glow yellow.

Something tells me that 'Drazh' means 'kill.'

That's a golem.

And I'm squishy.

Fuck.

I start to grab my shirt to pull it off, but the golem takes a step far faster than I'd like. No choice. Intent (and a little panic to help it along) call out my Shaar'Nath side. I go from looking up at the golem's face to looking down at it. My wings stretch out, my horns erupt, and I sprout claws. The main reason I decided to shift, the interlocking armor plates, are a damn sight better than learning what happens when stone golem fist meets unprotected flesh.

Eaves lets off a shriek like a little boy.

The golem swings its arm at me. I duck, and it comes around with a left. That, too, I avoid with a backward lean. When I pop back up, I punch it in the chest as hard as I can, knocking the thing off its feet. It goes sliding into Eaves' desk with a loud *slam*, bumping several things off the top. I glance at my knuckles, noting the lack of a broken hand. It didn't even hurt.

Awesome.

Eaves tosses another firebolt at me, but I make no effort to avoid it. The flames wash over me like a warm summer breeze. I snarl at him while stomping closer.

"Oh, hell no," says Lawrence from behind me. "I'm out."

I glance over my shoulder at him as he steps in, whirls, and goes right back into the hallway. He spins again and creeps into the room. "Amari? Is that... you?"

"Yeah. I'll explain later."

The golem breaks apart as whatever animating force held it together quits. I'm about to feel like a badass, but individual stones tumble over each other and slide upward, allowing the ponderous thing to stand back up by reconstructing itself. Damn. Guess those are more difficult to destroy than I thought.

Once it's upright again, the golem charges at me. I brace for impact and catch it by the arms, but go sliding backward, my toe claws gouging the floor. Eaves mutters something else and a fiery detonation occurs between me and the rock man, blasting us apart. The detonation hits me like a baseball bat striking an armored vest and almost (but not quite) knocks the wind out of me. I cough up smoke. If he aims that one better, he might hurt me from the impact force, but he doesn't need to know that.

"Idiot. You can't burn me." I'm sorely tempted to show him what a real firebolt looks like, but one, I need information, and two, I'm still an extreme novice at that. I'm not sure I can even get it to work in the middle of a fight yet, and it's *so* damn tiring.

Looking away from the golem long enough to verbally snipe at Eaves costs me a stone fist to the side of the head. I spin with the hit and take a few steps to the side before landing bent over the long table on the right, knocking two jars and a bunch of candles to the floor.

The golem lumbers up behind me, fist raised. Grunting, I push myself up into a spin and hammer the construct in the face. It totters backward, but keeps its balance. While it's occupied trying not to fall over, I claw at its chest, but leave only tiny white lines on the stone.

After landing a left hook across its cheek, I spot another glowing mark on its forehead. Unlike the one in the closet, this one's not a sigil. It's more like a word made of four non-English letters. Something clicks in my mind that Natalie said ages ago. Glyph magic lasts forever—unless something damages the carving/painting/ink.

I lunge in at it, punching it in the chest with my left as a distraction while raking my claws at its forehead.

"No!" shouts Eaves, and mutters something arcane.

I try to keep him in sight while pressing my attack on the golem's forehead. It pounds me in the shoulder, which knocks me to one knee. My arm throbs, but it's still attached. The instant I stand again, a metallic clatter comes from Eaves' direction.

Black chains sheathed in green light fly like serpents from his outstretched hands and coil around me, pinning my arms. An odd sense of heaviness presses on my mind, probably from the eerie green glow, but whatever it's trying to do, the effect is only a mild, annoying distraction. The golem grabs me, clamping its stony hands over my arms where the bundle of chain wraps over my elbows. It lifts me off my feet and starts trying to crush me. I can't reach its face anymore with my arms trapped, and all the strength I'm throwing at trying to break free isn't doing anything.

"Amari!" yells Lawrence.

The mage tosses a firebolt at him, but Lawrence hits the deck, suffering only a mild burn on the outside of his right arm.

I growl something inhuman, staring at the glowing letters on the golem's forehead.

Eaves disregards Lawrence and laughs at me. "Aha. Got you."

If only I could reach the damn glyph. I grunt, struggling to force my arms apart, but manage only to stalemate the golem trying to squeeze me to death. Pretty sure without that chain, I'm stronger than this thing. How warped is that? Something swats me in the leg.

Fuck. I'm an idiot.

I thrust my tail up between my legs, and jam the bladed tip straight into the middle of the golem's forehead, since it's holding me obligingly high off the ground. Orange sparks crackle around the lettering. Eaves' eyes go wide with alarm; he ducks behind his desk. Shit, this thing is going to explode, isn't it? At least it's stopped moving. I curl up in a ball and drive both feet into its chest, flinging it over backward while launching myself out of its grip.

We land at the same time, both flat on our backs.

Did I mention I *hate* being tied up? I hated it as a kid being arrested, and I hate it even more now when someone's trying to kill me. Scratching at the chains with my claws doesn't help, but I get a grip on one and yank hard while again pushing outward with my elbows. Straining becomes grunting, which advances to growling.

With a thunderbolt-like *crack*, the chain bursts into a spray of shrapnel, individual links flying everywhere. One by one, the glowy green aura around the ink-black chain bits fades away. The faint fogginess in my head clears.

Sparks shoot from the golem's head with greater intensity. Sensing imminent doom, I leap to my feet and rush toward the door, trying to put my body between Lawrence and death.

Boom.

The golem goes off like a bomb and a concussion wave hurls me forward. *Clunks* from stones hitting wood come from everywhere. *Clicks* from stone darts bouncing off my armored ass sound a lot closer. A few fleshy *thuds* emanate from my left and right along with a metric shitload of pain.

When I open my eyes, I find myself standing in the doorway, clinging by claws to the doorjamb. My wings, stretched out to either side, are functionally stapled to the walls through the thin membrane by several dozen stone daggers. Holy crap this hurts. I think I'm crying.

What sucks even more is that I know I can't stand here vulnerable, especially with my back to the mage. I chant 'I will heal' over and over in my head a few times before bracing against the doorframe and pushing myself backward. The stone shards stay put, firmly planted in the wood, but wing membrane pulls off them, every wound widening and scraping. My leathery bits tear in a few places. The pain is so bad, I let out an anguished roar. The last two, farthest at the edges, bring more tears to my eyes when they rip loose, and I'm free.

My roar seems to have stunned Craig and left Lawrence with his hands clamped over his ears. I stomp across the room and pick the mage up by a two-fisted grip of his pink button-down shirt. I'm definitely stronger in this form. Maybe I could've thrown that Civic across the street like this. Lifting this guy isn't even taxing.

"Where's Morris?" I growl. "And if I even think you're trying to invoke magic, I'm going to tear your arms off."

Eaves shakes.

I bump him into the wall a few times to jog his memory.

"I don't know. Morris is only the guy who brought me the crystal to work on and picked it up after. I did the job as a favor to Vittorino because I thought it would be helpful to have them friendly later on. I have no idea why they wanted it or what they intended to burn with it."

Lawrence, still a bit dazed, walks over. He gives me another wide-eyed stare before swatting dust out of his hair. "It all circles back to Michael. Sad thing is, this guy's not really all that involved, but he's probably going to go down harder. Unless the Mob pays him back that favor with a lawyer. Oh, and he did try to kill you."

Craig emits a strangled laugh. "You're not going to take this to court. They'll be as sympathetic to you as they are to magic users."

"Now what?" I ask.

Lawrence pulls out his phone. "Now, we write a detailed report. We're not the police. We have no powers of arrest."

"This guy tried to kill me!" I shake the mage until he gurgles.

"Technically, the golem tried to kill you," mutters Craig.

"Firebolts? That exploding thing?" I shake my head. "Directed attack."

"That you're immune to," parries Craig, sounding a bit more confident. "It's not a threat to you, so it won't count for charges."

Lawrence moans. "I hate arcane shit. The law's so damn muddy. Does intent count even if it had no way to harm you?"

"He made the golem, and he told it to *drazh* me. And I don't think that's Czechoslovakian for 'make her a nice tea and biscuit.' The golem existed by his magic so it counts—"

"*Azhdre Morh!*" shouts Craig.

Before the words 'I'm gonna rip his arms off' can even form in my head, a blinding white flash accompanies an explosion that hurls me off my feet. The next thing I know, I'm lying on my back with quite a bit of former house laying on top of me. Beams, some shingles, a couple boards.

I'm sore, but nothing *hurts*.

"Oh, that's it. This isn't even going to make it to court." I fling the beam off and stand.

Craig's sprawled on the deck outside by the pool, arms and legs spread like he's making a snow angel. A potion bottle held only by his lips drains a cherry-red liquid into his mouth. That bottle's about to go into another hole.

I make it three steps toward him before a pained moan emanates from the room behind me.

Lawrence lays curled up on his side clutching a broom handle-sized shard of wood that's impaled him in the gut and sticks out his back. He looks like he got into a fistfight with a pack of bears and lost. I can't even count the cuts.

"Oh, crap." I run to him. "Lawrence!"

Craig wobbles to his feet and spits the potion bottle to the side. Gripping his right thigh, he limp-runs around the pool, scurrying off into the trees.

"Get him," wheezes Lawrence. "I'm okay."

I watch Craig for two seconds before taking a knee by Lawrence. "No. You're not."

17

MERCY FLIGHT

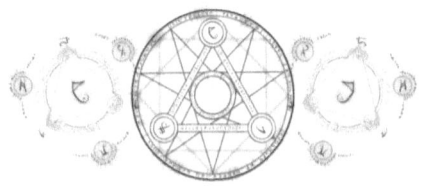

I can't let Lawrence die. Someone can track down Eaves later on, but if I don't do something *now*, Lawrence will never wind up sipping funny-colored drinks on a Florida beach. I've had enough training to know that yanking out a giant impaling object like that will only hurt him more. That's for the doctors and/or Lifemages to do. I shorten it with my claws to make it easier to move him at least.

As gently as I can, I get my arms under him and lift. "Hang on, man. I'm gonna get you to help."

He moans past gritted teeth. Seeing him in agony fans my rage, but I have to stuff it back down. If I ever find Eaves again, he's not going to need to worry about what a judge thinks of him.

"Sorry if this hurts a little."

Again, Lawrence moans.

I jog a few steps while stretching my wings. When I leap into the air, he stifles a wail. My flight is magical in nature and the wings are more of a steering mechanism-slash-parachute. In my fully-shifted form, it feels like I'm even stronger in regard to flying. When I carried Dunn out of the hotel, I hadn't understood anything about how it worked. Now that I've had some practice, carrying a grown man is no big deal.

The sun makes it relatively easy to steer east toward Philadelphia, and I pour as much desire as I can into going fast. A chilly gale hits me in the face like I'm on a motorcycle without a windscreen, but it doesn't get in the way of me seeing. Habit makes my wings beat every so often, but mostly, I glide on air currents and magic.

A few minutes after we're underway, he passes out.

"Come on, Lawrence. Stay with me. You're gonna make it."

He doesn't react.

Grief tears dribble out of the corners of my eyes, forced back over my cheeks in the wind.

"You still got ten years left before you can retire. Florida beaches and those weird drinks, man."

A weak smile appears on his face.

Whew.

I lean into the flight, trying to claw and scrape up every scrap of speed I can find. All the while, I keep talking about Florida, or babble about how I think I'm half-human and half-something from another plane.

"I know you don't like magic and enchanted things, but you don't need to be afraid of me. Don't worry about anything but staying with me, okay? We're hauling ass. I think I can outrun a medical helicopter. I'm gonna get you to Temple U Hospital."

He murmurs a not-word.

"Forget Craig. I'm not letting you die."

A glimmer of gold-white off to the left rises up from the ground and angles toward us. For a moment, I wonder if someone fired a surface-to-air missile at us, but as the comet draws closer, I make out the form of a blonde woman with white, feathered wings, the source of the dazzling light.

Mythology associates angels with healing, but Elestari aren't angels. I also don't have time to waste on another prissy, stuck-up snob right now.

The Elestari gains on us with enough ease that I get worried. Are they better in the air, or is carrying Lawrence slowing me down that much?

"What are you doing?" shouts the woman once she's closed enough distance to be heard.

Her eyes are gemstone red, and radiate light like mine though they still look human. She's about my age, has a skimpy white toga-like garment that covers her breasts and body, extending down her legs enough to hide her naughty bits—as long as she doesn't bend at all.

I ignore her, continuing to focus on speed.

The Elestari pulls up alongside and enough above me that our wings don't smack together. She seems to be flapping a lot more.

"You're being reckless," she shouts. "Someone will see you! Your kind are always so impetuous."

Shoot me now. She sounds like a spoiled rich girl throwing a wobbly over a store running out of perfume.

The woman gasps. "And what are you doing with that human? That's cruel!" She pulls a slender sword, also silver-and-gold, out of thin air and points it at me. "I'm not going to let you drag him off to wherever you're taking him to finish your evil work. Put him down this instant."

I blink. I guess what they say about blondes has some truth to it. "You do realize we're like five hundred feet up. If I drop him... Look, sweetie, I don't give a fuck about being obvious right now. Lawrence is going to die, and I have to get him to a hospital. If someone sees me, oh well."

"What?" She gawks at me. The sword dissipates in a flash of sparkles. "You're *helping* him?"

"Yes, I'm helping him. I'm not like you. They're not ants to me."

The girl pouts. "We're not *all* like that. Some of us take care of the humans. They're so cute and defenseless. You're really his friend?"

"Yes." I roll my—no I don't. My eyes are glowing pools of energy. Can't really roll them.

"I'm Laniah." She holds out a hand.

I disregard her offer to shake—mostly because I can't—and keep flying.

Gold light swells into a sphere upon her palm, and she throws it into Lawrence's chest. Some of his smaller cuts disappear.

Oh, she wasn't offering a handshake.

"That should keep him until you can get to a Lifemage," says Laniah. "What's your name?"

Really? She's trying to be BFFs now? A minute ago, she wanted to stab me.

"Brooklyn."

"Nice to meet you. Sorry about assuming." Laniah waves and pulls off to the left.

She goes into a steep dive, and soon becomes a comet of light, too far away to make out her body. Well, that was special. Lawrence is still breathing, which makes me feel somewhat better.

Philadelphia is obvious from the air. I know the approximate location of Temple University Hospital, and a giant, tall building stands out. As soon as I spot it, I zero in on the square, white helipad on the roof and dive.

There's no one up here, which gives me a moment of surprising relief. Naked is a lot easier to explain than being a seven-and-a-half foot tall critter with horns, wings, and a tail, so I shift back to human form as soon as we touch down. Not even my boots survived the explosion. Well, no time to worry about that now.

I run down a ramp from the helipad, which hooks a right angle turn by a wall and continues to a heavy, automatic door on the left. Sorry for not radioing in before landing. I use my foot to hit the metal button beside the door, which opens on a mechanical arm, and rush in carrying Lawrence. Even in my normal form, he's not much of a burden.

The hallway opens into a receiving area and an elevator on the left. A single man staffs a desk, and he looks up with a startled expression.

"Lawrence needs help. We got caught in an explosion."

He mashes his hand on something out of sight and holds a phone to his ear. "Need a doctor and a trauma team at the helipad, stat."

"Hang on, man," I whisper to Lawrence. "We're at the hospital. You're gonna be okay."

"How'd you get on the roof?" asks the guy behind the desk.

I look up from Lawrence and make eye contact with the man. "It was a big explosion."

18

REAL EVIDENCE

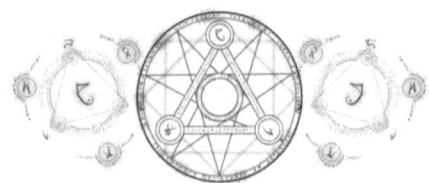

I wind up warming a bed in the hospital for about an hour after their security staff asked me to stay. Since I don't look injured and I'm not complaining about anything, I get the 'she can wait' treatment. Eventually, a doctor walks in. People only see Lifemages if they're as messed up as Lawrence. Mostly, doctors deal with the minor stuff, except in more rural areas where there aren't any mages.

"So, it says here you somehow wound up on the roof naked?" He looks up from his e-tablet. "And blamed an explosion?"

I pick at the hem of the hospital gown they gave me. "I think you ought to give that guy a brain scan. His sense of humor isn't working."

The doctor grins, stifling a laugh. "All right, so how *did* you wind up on the roof?"

"How's Lawrence?"

"As far as I know, still in surgery."

"Wait? Surgery? No mage?" I lean forward, mouth open in surprise.

"His condition wasn't that severe." The doctor pulls up a chair and sits. "The mages usually take care of missing limbs, failing organs, cancer, genetic defects, that sort of thing. Issues that doctors cannot address, or when doing so would require pain and suffering as bad or worse than the condition."

"Oh. I thought they did everything big." I swish my feet side to side. "Good to know. And I'm not hurt. The explosion was magical in nature, and about all it did to me was blast my clothes off."

His expression shifts to concern. "That's an odd effect. Were you attacked?"

"Yeah, but not like that. It wasn't a perv. I don't understand how magic works really." I explain how Lawrence and I went out to this place to interview a suspect in an arson investigation, who turned out to be a mage. I'm mostly honest except for my shape-change. In the version I tell the doctor, I got a hold of a dagger and gouged the golem after a few close calls ducking its fists. "I found an enchanted feather that gave me wings when I used it, but they disappeared when I landed."

He nods, adding notes to a file on his e-tablet. The usual questions follow: do I feel strange, headache, dizziness, soreness, etc. After that, he checks my eyes and heart rate, and declares me fit.

"Great. So, I'm all set then. How long is Lawrence going to be in surgery? When can I come back and see him?"

"We can't release you just yet," says the doctor.

"Why not?"

"We need to confirm your claim of who you are first. You must admit showing up on the roof in the nude with a severely-injured man raises a multitude of questions."

I sigh. "My wallet and cell are in the woods somewhere in the wreckage of that house... if they haven't been vaporized. Is there a phone I can use?"

"Sure." He stands and calls in the security officer who'd been outside my door the whole time.

"Dave'll bring you to a phone," says the doctor.

"Thanks." I hop out of bed and follow the hospital cop to an empty nurse's station a short distance down the corridor. My ass is on display for the world, but I don't care.

He points at a phone. "Dial nine for an outside line."

"Thanks." I call my stationhouse.

"Engine 53," says Kenny.

"Hey, Kenny. It's Brooklyn."

"Oh, hey, FMO girl. What's up?"

I hold back the sigh. "I'm at the hospital with Lawrence. I need to talk to Lieutenant Sims."

"Oh, shit. You okay?" asks Kenny.

"Yeah, I'm fine, but Lawrence is in surgery."

"Oh wow. Poor guy. Hold on. Let me check if Sims is free."

The line cuts to silence with a click.

"Amari?" asks Sims, about twenty seconds later. "What's going on?"

"I'm at Temple University Hospital. Lieutenant Lawrence Ellis from the Fire Marshal's Office got hurt pretty bad. A mage attempted to kill us by setting off an explosion. I don't have any ID with me and they think I'm nuts. Can you please show up here and tell them I am who I say I am?"

"All right. Give me a couple minutes. I'll call Captain Greene and let her know her guy's in bad shape. How's he doing?"

I explain his condition as best I can, given what I remember.

"Damn. Hope he pulls through," says Sims.

"Yeah." I choke up a little. "Me too."

After hanging up, I follow the hospital cop back to my room. We wind up talking shop for a while, and I get the sense he believes I'm not a nutjob, since we know a lot of the same names from the fire department and EMT crowd.

Lieutenant Sims arrives about forty minutes later. He also gets the magic trinket gave me temporary wings story. Like most people who aren't users of magic, he reacts to it with 'bah, magic was involved, whatever you say.' I'm out the door in borrowed clothes soon after, and Sims is kind enough to give me a ride home.

He clears his throat when I open the SUV door. "Do you know if this temporary thing is ongoing or will you be back with us tomorrow? Only asking so I know if I can tell you to take the day off and get some rest. That's quite a story."

I pause with one foot on the ground, one on the running board. "I don't really know. We tracked down the guy who made the incendiary device, and got some names, but the mage got away, Lawrence got hurt, and the names we *did* get are all part of organized crime. It's the police's turn for this one, I think. We know how the fire started, and have a good guess why."

He nods. "All right. As far as I'm concerned, you're back with us then, so I want you to take tomorrow and collect yourself. If anyone from the FMO gives you shit, send them to me."

"Thanks, Ell-tee."

"Wednesday?" he asks.

"Yeah. See you then." I smile and shut the door.

After a trudge up six flights of stairs, I stagger to my apartment and stare at the locked door. My keys are somewhere in a house in the woods. Dammit. I really wanted my bed.

I grumble my way back down the stairs and go outside before taking the fire escape to the roof. It's getting dark now, so my tolerance for care is weak. After peeling off the charity Temple University sweatshirt they gave me, I let my wings out and zip off into the air. I'm beginning to understand why all those paintings of angels and succubi are always bare-chested. It's *such* a pain in the ass to have to keep taking my shirt off and putting it back on.

It only takes a few minutes to fly back to Martin Bradstreet's apartment, a much quicker trip than heading all the way out to that damn house again. Landing in an alley nearby affords me the chance to put the hoodie back on and walk like a normal person. I'm like twenty steps from the entrance to the apartment building's parking lot when the *bwoop* of a police siren startles me into a statue. That sound scares me more than normal startlement. It snuck up on me a lot as a kid, and it usually ended with me getting a new pair of bracelets, but that didn't bother me as much as the long, disappointed talks from Mom.

Once the paralytic shock wears off, I look over my shoulder at a pair of officers rolling by slow in their patrol car.

"You should get inside as fast as possible, ma'am," says a guy that can't be older than nineteen. "There's a bear roaming around."

I blink. Oh, whew. I'm not in trouble. "A bear?"

"Yeah. Totally serious," says the driver, a fortyish guy with a few grey hairs and extra pounds. "No damn idea how a freakin' bear gets into Philly, but we got a ton of reports and some pictures."

I think I know how a bear got into Philly. We left the damn portal open. Oops.

"Thanks." I point at the apartment building. "I'll go right inside."

They both wave at me and drive off.

It's almost funny, but that poor bear is probably scared.

As expected, the apartment is still empty. I don't feel like dealing with the back and forth of bugging the super, so I press on the door until it breaks open. The rug and sofa are shredded. White fluff has scattered all over the floor and it looks like the bear broke out a window. Probably jumped since it's only the second floor. Curiosity gets the better of me and I peer down.

Below the window, a pile of trash bags has exploded all over the sidewalk and the street. Hard to say if he landed on them and they popped or if he shredded them after touchdown. Probably a bit of both. With a shrug, I push off the windowsill and head to the bedroom.

Fortunately, the portal's still open. I step through into the woods and decide to strip and leave these clothes behind in case Craig has come back or he's left some other nasty surprise. I wad the sweatshirt and jeans around the cheap sneakers and stash them behind a tree. Right now, all I want to do is go home and crawl in bed, though I doubt I'll get much sleep worrying about Lawrence.

I storm through the woods to the house, which appears to be abandoned. Squatting behind a pine, I watch for a good five minutes, and nothing moves. The forest is silent, save for the ambient din of wildlife at night. Good. Since I'd rather not step barefoot on sharp shit, I shift fully. Yes, the armor even covers the bottoms of my feet. It also seems to be covering everything other than my face too. How do full Shaar'Nath pee? Or procreate? I wonder if the armor's something they can 'take out or put away' as needed?

Experimentation can wait.

A while of rummaging around in the debris makes me a happy girl. My pants wound up on the floor as soon as I got angry enough to stop caring about who saw me as a 'demon,' so they weren't exposed to the brunt of Craig's final-fuck-you explosion. My phone survived! I grab my wallet as well as my keys and leave, crunching over smashed boards, broken glass, and shattered drywall. Pity; this house looked expensive.

Before long, I'm dressed and back through the portal. Hmm. How do I close it from this side? The wall with the symbol became the doorway. Oh, there it is. It moved to the right. One finger poke and the rear of the closet solidifies. No more bears.

If there's anything useful at that house, the cops can deal with it.

MY CELL PHONE WAKES ME UP BY HAVING THE AUDACITY TO RING AT nine the next morning. I don't recognize the number, so I ignore it. It rings again as soon as it stops. Ugh. Fine. Persistent bastard.

"Hello?" I croak.

"Am I speaking to Brooklyn Amari?" asks a woman who sounds on the older side.

"Yes."

"Hello, Miss Amari. This is Captain Evelyn Greene of the Fire Marshal's Office."

I sit up. Shit. "Good morning, captain. Sorry. Had a rough night. Lieutenant Sims told me to take the day."

"That's fine. Would you feel up to meeting with me a little later this morning at my office?"

She doesn't sound pissed, so I try not to panic too much. "Of course, ma'am. What time should I be there?"

"Eleven is fine," says Captain Greene.

"Yes, ma'am. I'll be there."

"Talk to you then."

I stare at the blank screen for a couple of minutes. Eventually, my panic fades. Greene is Lawrence's boss. She's probably going to ask questions about what happened. Crap! Lawrence. I hunt down the number for the hospital, but no one will give me any information about him since I'm not a relative. "Come on, dammit, I'm with the fire department. I was ten feet away from him when he got hurt" gets me put on hold.

"Miss Amari?" asks a confident male voice.

"Yes." Is my life on repeat?

"I'm Doctor Rao. I understand you're with the fire department?"

"That's right. I'm the one who brought him in. We were working together at the time he was hurt."

The doctor clears his throat. "I can tell you that he's out of surgery and resting now. We expect he'll make a full recovery, though he will likely be here for a few weeks."

My heart swells. "Oh, thank you. When will he be able to have visitors?"

"Probably tonight or tomorrow at the earliest. Might want to plan for tomorrow since he's on a good deal of painkillers right now."

"Okay, thanks."

"Have a good day," says the doctor.

Whew. I flop back on my bed and stare at the ceiling.

THE SHOES OF MY DRESS UNIFORM CLICK DOWN A LONG CORRIDOR IN City Hall, echoing off the marble. Captain Greene's office sits near the end on the left. It's smaller than I expected, but still nice. A portrait of the mayor hangs on the wall behind her, and her bookshelves are full of important-looking tomes as well as small statues and fire service kitsch. The captain's edging up on fifty. She looks good for her age. Thick, greying hair hangs straight to her shoulders, framing an angular face of deep brown.

Peering in the door, I ask, "Ma'am?"

"Please, sit." She gestures at one of the two chairs facing her desk.

I walk over and take a seat.

"How is Lawrence?"

"I haven't had a chance to see him yet, but I called the hospital. They said he's resting now, but won't be able to have visitors until tomorrow."

She nods, her grim expression relaxing. "I wanted to thank you for saving his life."

"It wasn't a choice, ma'am." To keep myself from fidgeting, I clamp my hands over my knees.

"I understand the man who you went to interview fled the scene, also injured."

"That's correct, ma'am. Catching him was not worth Lawrence's life."

Captain Greene stares at her desk in solemn silence for a moment. "I've been reading over the investigation notes for this case. Our official opinion is that Michael Rossellini conspired with at least two other individuals, Ronald Harris and this mage—"

"Craig Eaves," I add.

She clicks a computer mouse a few times, gazing at her screen. "That's not in the file, but of course it isn't. Lieutenant Ellis would've been doing this. You don't have access."

"There's also the bartender at Otto's." I explain my theory that Michael contacted that man who put him in touch with either Ronald or Craig. I'm still fuzzy if there is a Ronald Harris or if that had been a disguised Craig. Eaves said Harris brought him the crystal, but that could've been BS.

"We're quite certain this has connections to organized crime." Captain Greene scowls. "All we can do is put together the most solid evidence possible. Going after them is for the police and the courts. We've established the cause of the fire and have the device. That is our responsibility here."

"Yes, ma'am."

"Might I ask why you decided to go confront this Mr. Eaves in person instead of referring it to the police?"

"Magic was involved, ma'am." I explain the portal in the empty apartment. "Once I activated the portal, I expected Eaves would become aware that it had been opened. I thought that by the time we involved the police, he'd either be long gone, or the department's policy on magic-users would complicate the investigation."

"Which policy would that be?" asks Captain Greene.

"Umm, the 'eek, it's a mage, kill it' policy." I offer a weak smile. "Especially once he revealed himself as a Pyromancer."

"Hmm." She rubs her chin. "And why did this man attack you?"

"Because we cornered him. I'm… a little psychic, ma'am. Psychometry, it's how I found a lot of it so far. When I confronted Eaves, I knew enough that he became frightened the Mob would kill him. Someone named Ernesto… I don't know if 'Ernesto' is a hitman or a boss."

Captain Greene grins. "Must be dangerous if his mere name made a Pyromancer mess his pants."

Oh, that was me. I smile to myself.

"Lieutenant Ellis had a recorder going during your meeting, but right around the time that statue starts moving, the video and audio become static. Did something happen at that moment?"

"Maybe the golem was giving off some kind of interference. It kind of had *all* my attention. Eaves may have done something I didn't notice." I'm easy enough with lies that it flows with little effort. And here I thought my skill came from being a teenager. It's been a couple years since I needed to hurl a false-itude that big. I hope it doesn't bite me in the ass. So wow, I mess with cameras when I change. Good to know.

"Bah. Magic," says Captain Greene.

My smile turns sad. "Lawrence says that a lot."

"That he does. I've got an email here from him speaking highly of you in regards to an open position with my department."

I nod. "I've been considering it."

"While we may be able to bend certain requirements given your paranormal talents, the position does require a basic level of competence with arson investigation."

There goes that. "Umm. I guess Lawrence was expecting me to jump in and hit the ground running, learn while doing."

She smiles. "That may still be on the table, if he's up to taking on a probationary understudy. The open slot with the investigative team is the primary for handling matters involving arcane or unexplainable phenomena. Applicants are not exactly beating down the door."

"Yeah," I say, looking down.

After what happened, Lawrence may have had his fill of it. A month from now, he could be in Florida on the beach. I don't know why the thought of that disappoints me. Maybe I *do* want the transfer. Going back to school in my downtime to study arson investigation sounds like a drag. I'm not sure I'd chase the transfer if I had to do that—I'm happy pulling people out of burning buildings.

I'm starting to think that's a lot safer.

"Thank you for the advice. I'm still trying to make up my mind."

Captain Greene smiles. "Of course. You're young yet. You've got time. I imagine we will eventually find someone, so if you decide to pursue it, don't wait *too* long."

"Thank you, ma'am."

"And by the way, a psychometrist would be an enormous help. Quite a bit easier to figure out what happened when you're watching it unfold instead of studying burn patterns."

I think she wants me to put in for the interview. Erk. I better make up my mind. "Yeah."

"What's it like?" she asks, oddly casual.

Her shift in tone from commander to curious relaxes me. I lapse into a description of how it felt to see Ronald plant the crystal. The whole time, Captain Greene stares at me like a young girl enthralled by a spooky campfire story. I shouldn't read too much into that, but I do get the sense she likes me and hopes I want the job.

But, going back to school, bleh. The thought of it fills me with the same loathing I had as a teenager. At least if I go, they'd better pay for the classes.

19

THE ARMISTICE

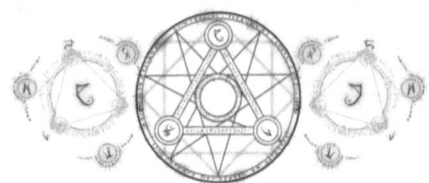

T he following day, I stop in at the hospital to see Lawrence around eleven in the morning. He's still out cold, but no longer appears to be knocking on death's door. The rich, brown hue is back to his face and his breathing has lost the wheeziness. I cringe at the sight of a drain tube coming out of his side to a tank of reddish-brown fluid. That giant stick had to have pierced a lung.

I sit nearby and talk randomly about this and that, mostly Captain Greene's apparent nudging for me to put in for the arson investigation unit. If I got it, I'd be the youngest person ever, but I worry about my lack of credentials creating legal issues down the road. Some slick defense attorney could turn it into a 'he-said-she-said' if all I've got to go on is whatever vision I claim to have seen.

Maybe I'm thinking about it wrong. I wouldn't be standing up there pointing at someone and yelling 'they did it because I saw it.' No, I'd use the visions like breadcrumbs to lead me to tangible evidence... like I did with the Rossellini case. Only that didn't exactly work out. That's why I'm hesitating. I'm pissed off at Eaves, and frustrated that even with being able to grab stuff and see visions, I couldn't hand the police enough to let them go after anyone.

"I'm gonna find that bastard, Lawrence." I sigh and mutter, "With or without cops."

A while later, he wakes up long enough to call me 'nurse' a few times and babble incoherently about how much he doesn't want me to let it rain tomorrow. Wow, he's high as hell. They must've given him the good stuff. I get him some water and attempt to have a conversation, but he can't seem to wrap his brain around my not being a nurse or having powers of weather control.

Once he falls asleep again, I decide to let him rest.

Eaves' face hovers in my thoughts on the way along the corridor. Part of me wants to hunt him down and rip him in half, but the other part that Mom's responsible for recoils at the idea of simply killing everyone who pisses me off. Yeah, that's probably not a good idea—except in cases like Frank. Guess I'll do the cat thing... chase the rat and bring him back alive as a present for Philadelphia's finest.

A LITTLE AFTER FIVE THAT EVENING, I'M SQUATTING AT THE FRONT END of our pump truck giving the chrome bits some love with a rag and polish. It's not like I've been here for years, but the stationhouse feels like home. The arson investigation unit is tempting and scary all at once, an unusual sensation for me as I usually plunge into things with little care. At least I've come to understand why fire calls to me. Maybe I should tell Mom how I really survived when our trailer burned. Nah. She hates even thinking about that night since she believes I almost died. Would it help her handle it if I explained it's not possible for me to die by fire? Meh, hell with it. No sense picking that scab.

Someone walks up behind me, not an uncommon occurrence at the stationhouse, so I don't give it much attention save for a quick glance back at a set of man's legs in black BDU pants. Another dab of polish on the cloth, I attack the feed pipe cap right in the middle of the truck's nose.

"Hey," says Jason.

I freeze.

"I'm really sorry about the other night. I... can't even explain what happened."

"Jason..." I grab the bumper for balance and stand out of my squat.

He's got his hands stuffed in his pockets and stares down like a scolded puppy. "I keep seeing that weird dude, and there's all this light around him, and... I remember being so fucking scared. Worse than I'd ever felt about my father."

So, David Graf, bartender at Niflheim, *did* whammy him with some kind of fear spell. Being able to feel others' intentions is awesome for avoiding unnecessary arguments. It's a giant stone weight off my heart to learn he wasn't afraid of *me*.

I step closer and take his hand. "It's not your fault. That guy used magic to make you go away. And no, he's *not* a rival. His looks are perfect, but he's a complete asshole."

Jason laughs, smiles, and stumbles over a word or five. Guess he wasn't expecting me to forgive him so easily. Really, he didn't do anything but get victimized by an Elestari with magic.

"And yes. I'd love to go out again with you. Maybe Friday night?"

"You're amazing." He leans in closer, going for a kiss.

Hell with it. I grab on, and we kiss like the world no longer exists, right there in front of the truck. It doesn't take long for a few wiseasses to clap. Having an audience kills the mood for him, but I ignore them. He pulls back, blushing and trying to play it off like he's not embarrassed.

"I've gotta do something tonight for that investigation, but I'll call you as soon as I can, okay?" I grin.

I love the way his eyes light up in reaction to my smile.

He caresses my cheek, gives me a light peck on the lips, and gestures at the pumper. "Want a little help?"

"Heh sure." I toss him a spare rag from the box. Cleaning a fire truck together isn't what most girls think of as romantic, but I'm not most girls.

It's a few minutes past eleven that night when I glide down out of the sky and land by the wreckage of the exploded house. My racer-back shirt gives my wings plenty of space, but it does crap against a cold breeze. I wonder if my Shaar'Nath nipples could cut steel right now. As soon as I'm down, I put the wings away and pull on the sweat-jacket I carried.

No need for a full shift as combat boots handle walking around busted up house just fine, but I think my work BDU pants are loose enough to survive my armor coming out without too much damage except for where the tail breaks free. At least, unless some idiot Pyromancer tries to kill me with a giant explosion again.

Wandering around the wreckage hunting for clues is a lot more boring than I thought it would be. Flying is safer at night (harder to see me) but one thing my supernatural heritage lacks is night vision. I should've brought a damn flashlight.

Frustrated, I stand in the middle of the carnage, arms folded. I need to learn more about being what I am. Hmm. On a whim, I close my eyes and try to mentally call out to my father. He did say he'd watched me my whole life, so—I blink. Did *I* kill that guy in the car when I was ten? Or was that dad?

"You're welcome," says Dad.

He appears out of thin air behind me, still wearing an expensive black suit, the collar of his white shirt open. I love the way he's not-quite-smiling, like he got away with something illegal. Great. I have the most interesting dad in the world.

"You did that?"

He nods. "Though, you did give the bastard a headache."

"Can I kill people like that? I mean… whatever that was?"

"With enough practice, if you should choose." He walks up and puts an arm around me. "The same way you use your mind to lift things. It's like a hand reaching into the skull and crushing the brain. You have plenty of strength to do it, but the difficult part is the control."

Oh, wow. I grew up thinking I'd killed a guy when I was ten years old, but I'd been more freaked out that doing it didn't freak me out.

Guess my kill count is down to one. By the way, bus guy survived. And you know what's really messed up? His pal died during the commission of a crime, so they're charging *him* with murder. Is it bad of me to find that hilarious?

"You're about to ask for help, yes?" asks Dad.

I gesture around at the rubble. "I want to find a mage." I explain what happened, the fire, the Mob, and this guy almost killing Lawrence.

"Hunting a mage, hmm? Usually, they are the ones who summon us." He winks.

"Are you serious?" I stare at him. "I thought you said we weren't demons?"

Dad paces around, nudging bits of wood or drywall with his foot. "We're not. At least not in the sense that humans believe in demons. However, some magic is capable of summoning beings like us who are not native to the Armistice."

"An armistice is a truce."

"It's also what we call the mortal world." He winks. "The energy that was poured into creating it ties us all to it. Some mages have learned how to tap into that and pull our strings."

A shiver takes me. "So... they can control us?"

"Not in the sense you're fearing. Some can drag us out of our world into this one or create barriers we cannot cross, but they are incapable of dominating our minds or turning us into slaves."

"Oh, whew." When that fear fades, I grin. "Eaves had no idea what I am. He kept trying to burn me."

Dad throws back his head and laughs, spooking something off in the woods. Probably a deer.

Anger strikes me out of nowhere, at the Elestari for keeping him out of my life so long. Before the 'I want to kill them all' urge takes hold, the thought of Laniah (as irritating as she was at first) dispels it. Maybe they're not *all* sanctimonious assholes.

"Something bothering you, Brooklyn?" asks Dad.

"Only wishing I'd met you years ago." I kick at debris. "Would've helped a lot. Explained things."

He squeezes my shoulder. "Childhood is but a camera flash for us. We have plenty of time."

Huh what? "Wait? You're saying we're immortal?"

"Not totally. Most of us make it about ten thousand years or so. I don't know what effect your being part human will have on that."

"Wow. So I could stick around for anywhere from eighty years to holy shit."

Dad laughs again.

"So…" I guess I really can't let this go. "Mages can really summon us?"

"Not exactly… Think about it this way, if anyone speaks your true name, you will know it. Most of the time, those who believe they 'summon' us aren't doing anything more than asking us to come check out what they're up to."

"Oh. Wow, that makes so much sense. As a kid, I always knew when Mom was calling me."

"That's part of being a kid."

I glance at him. "No, I mean it. I like really *felt* something."

"Interesting. You consider Brooklyn your true name… it's not a usual Shaar'Nath name."

"I'm not a usual Shaar'Nath." I cross my arms and flash an impish smirk. "It's my name."

Dad smiles for a second before something gets his attention and he strides over to what had once been the corner of the room closest to the pool. Shattered glass from the sliding door coats the ground like a deadly version of winter frost. He crouches, tracing his fingers around the floor.

"Here."

I crunch over to stand next to him. "What?"

"This blood is from the man you wish to find," says Dad. "While our kind is not as often aligned with magic, there are a few techniques that remain available to us."

This sounds like it's going to turn dark in a hurry. I squat to get a better look at the spatters of dried blood. "Blood magic?"

"Of sorts. The darkness you're fearing is a different

implementation. Using someone else's blood to empower a curse upon them, or sacrificing your own for power is not the same. We can use blood to find the source. If you are still suffering from the human delusion of good and evil, merely locating someone is neither."

"Dad... good and evil aren't the illusion. It's all the other bullshit they associate with it. I don't need the fear of punishment in some mythical afterlife to know something's wrong. So, how does this work?"

He cocks his head, smiling that smile of a parent who thinks their kid said something stupid and cute. "For us, it is easier than humans. For you as well. Our nature contains vast amounts of energy that are sure to overwhelm the brittle human shell. Take some of the blood upon your fingertips."

"So, I'm not a half-human? More like a quarter?" I stick two fingers in the stain, but it's dry, so I use a little spit to help.

"You're trying to quantify the unquantifiable. What is the length of the water in a glass? How much does time weigh?" He grasps my hand, gazing at the red smears on the tips of my fingers. "This blood is connected to the soul it came from. Focus on it but not the stain. See it as a portal into another place. Ask your mind to lead you to the other end of the tunnel."

"Right. No funny words?"

He grins. "Not for us—or for the Elestari. Humans use the words to focus their thoughts so they can draw power from outside the Armistice. We are steeped in it."

My desire to find Eaves wells up. It takes some concentration to force myself to want to bring him in alive, but I do. After a few minutes of staring at my fingers, trying to see *through* the bloody spots, a flicker of light slides over them. My brain struggles to latch on to the energy teasing at me from within, but it's elusive.

"That's it. You're almost there," says Dad. "Think of the blood on your fingers as two tiny doors. Push them open."

Like trying to see one of those weird 3D pattern pictures, I let my eye focus extend past my fingertip, trying to peer into the blood spot as if it were an opening. The light strengthens, and both bloodstains glow bright red. In that instant, I become aware of Eaves' presence. It's a feeling of direction and distance, like how when someone walks up beside me, I can tell where they are.

"You're a fast student." Dad pats me on the back.

I lean against him, still gazing into what appear to be open bloody tunnels in my fingers. "All the credit goes to the teacher. Do I need to keep this blood on my fingers? How long will this last?"

"As long as you have the blood, until you stop wanting to find him, you find him, or about two hours after you wipe it off."

"Great." I wipe the blood off. "No sense wasting time. Thanks, Dad."

He pulls me into a stiff hug. "I'm never far away if you need me."

"Hey, it's not your fault. Sorry for being a little bitchy when you first showed up."

"And that's not *your* fault." He kisses me on the head like I'm a little girl. "You did not have enough information to understand."

"See you later, Dad."

He gives me an 'of course' bow, and fades away.

Now *that's* a neat trick. Maybe I'll ask him to teach me sometime.

As it turns out, I can fly pretty darn fast when not carrying someone. I again realize that I assumed something untrue. Shifting completely to my armored 'demon' form doesn't help me fly faster. Yes, I get stronger, but physical strength doesn't affect my flying since it's a magical effect. Without the armor plating, it feels like I'm going much faster due to less weight.

Following the sense leading me to Craig Eaves pulls me northeast. About twenty minutes after I leap into the air, the lights of New York City come into view. Damn. I'm hauling ass. That's gotta be a couple hundred miles per hour. Guess I don't need to worry about airport security, as long as I don't mind taking a redeye.

Or a blue-eye.

I had to shift them to be able to see against the high-speed wind.

The pull takes me to a high-rise hotel near the heart of the city. I circle the building a few times, zeroing in on the floor. Eventually, I catch sight of him in a room about two-thirds the way up. His room is bright, and his attention appears absorbed on the television, so I glide in for a silent landing on the balcony, which is tucked under the balcony of the next room above. This forces me into an awkward squat atop the railing while grabbing the underside of the concrete slab over my head. Since he didn't notice me, I step down and retract my wings back into black smoke wisps before pulling my hoodie on.

Eaves has his back to me, leaning both hands on a desk to the right of the television, which is off. What I'd thought to be the flickering glow of a TV is actually a baseball-sized crystal orb projecting a three-dimensional image of another man. It's almost like a Transpresence call, except the other person doesn't appear to be in the room with him. Expensive TP rigs even allow the users to touch each other—not to mention do other things long distance. Normal ones provide sight and sound only.

This mechanism is neither; he's speaking to a ghostly image of a robed figure, shown only from the chest up, with most of his face hidden by loose, violet silk.

What the hell is it with magic users and their robe fetish? Come on, people. Get with the times.

As soon as the guy hangs up, I'll rip the door off, knock him senseless, and carry his ass back to Philly. It is tempting to throw him out the patio and let gravity administer justice, but... Mom wouldn't approve. She might not even approve of what I did to Frank, but my mother is *too* nice.

"Setback?" shouts Eaves. "You call what happened a 'setback,' and expect me to carry on like nothing's changed."

The robed figure nods. "Exactly. This problem is one of your creation, Eaves. If you had been able to keep your temper in check, you would not be threatened. The mortal authorities have nothing. Or they had nothing until you attempted to kill two city employees."

"That bitch isn't human," roars Eaves. "You want to tell me what

I'm getting involved with? No one ever said anything about unfettered demons."

A haughty, condescending laugh comes from the projection. "That is most humorous. There is much left for you to learn. Fear not. Your assistance will not go unrewarded. However, it might be in your best interest to distance yourself from the mortals' petty criminals."

"Wait a moment." Eaves stands up straight, one finger raised. "You're talking about unmaking the entire world and you want me to stay calm?"

"Yes." The robed figure smiles. "In its current form, what you know as the human world is enabling the uncivilized to propagate their evil. It is a barrier that must be removed so we can eradicate the darkness. You need not worry. Another realm can be built for humanity, free of evil and temptation. Your kind's existence was unexpected, and this world you know was not designed properly to sustain living beings. We can create a much more suitable environment. You shall help herald a new era for your kind, in fact reshape humanity itself. Harmony and light shall replace discord and greed."

"That sounds both impossible and too good to be true," says Eaves. "Though I think you believe it."

"I believe it because I have seen worlds with such beauty, your limited abilities of communication do not enable me to adequately convey their majesty. Simple oscillations of sound cannot compare to sharing the visual, emotional, and spiritual presence. Oh, and you have a guest."

Craig spins to stare at me when the robed figure points.

Shit.

I leap to my feet and yank open the sliding door, snapping the lock. Eaves whirls back to face the glowing orb and raises his hands, chanting. The image of the robed figure sinks back into a growing indigo vortex with wavering edges, rising and expanding to become a doorway. I sprint for him, screaming as I strain to run faster than his portal spell can form.

The instant the bottom of the expanding gate touches the carpet, my hand slaps down on the orb projecting it. Without thinking, I unsheathe my claws and crush. A twinkle of shattering crystal fills the room, many times louder than such a delicate sound ought to be.

Eaves lets out a horrible scream.

I glance back at him; his head, one arm, and some of his chest is through the portal, but he's gone motionless as if frozen in time. The orb flashes like a dying light bulb, and explodes, leaving me without fingers on my right hand.

Before I can even feel that, Eaves pops. Blood and tiny pieces of mage spray everywhere.

Oops.

My missing fingers knock on my brain. Hello. Massive amount of pain calling.

I fall in place, cradling my hand to my chest and biting back a scream. Compared to having my wings stapled to the wall, this isn't too bad on the pain meter. Half a minute or so later, roots of pink flesh grow out of the stumps, twisting and stretching back to their normal length. The mesmerizing display captivates me until they've thickened and become fingers again.

They're somewhat stiff when flexed, and tender like I'd recently slammed them in a door, but the crippling pain is over. Out of nowhere, I get a sudden craving for a cheeseburger. Must be an aftereffect of healing myself. I sit up, covered in Eaves. The room looks like a red-lens photograph. He's been reduced to a fine crimson mist, plus a few stray bits.

Ugh. This is nasty.

I can't burn this out, not in a hotel with hundreds of people. Showering, though tempting, might leave DNA behind. Then again, I already did that with wherever my fingers went, but it's probably too mixed into liquid Eaves to be isolated. A shower drain would be obvious. The last thing I need is to be linked to an exploding mage, especially an exploding mage I have a motive to want dead. Even if I had been trying *not* to kill him. Oh well.

"That's for Lawrence." I kick a piece of him the size of a grape across the room.

Better get out of here before someone comes to check on all the noise.

A running leap sends me over the patio railing. I yank off my hoodie and sprout wings in mid free-fall, pulling up and climbing well out of the glare of the city lights, into the cover of a dark night sky.

Some distance off to the west in a suburban area, I land in a backyard with a nice, big pool. Motion activated lights chase me off, cursing under my breath. The fifth house I try has an even bigger pool, and no automatic lights. It's easier to explain soaking wet than covered in blood and gore. With my phone and keys safe on land, I fall, fully dressed, into the pool, and slosh around until I stop leaving blood trails in the water.

Dripping, but free of blood, I snag my stuff from the patio table, pop wings, and zip back into the air to head home. Not a drop of Eaves' blood is coming with me. Hell, it's not even leaving New York.

20

THE LAMEST DEMON

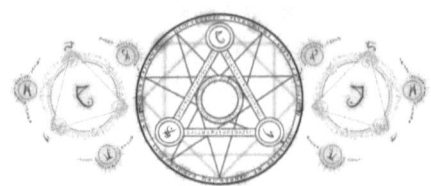

Saturday morning, I lay in bed with little desire to move. I stayed up late both Thursday and Friday night with Jason. Thursday, we hit a few bars and caught an indie band, and last night, we burned the candle at both ends in my apartment on the PlayStation. We even wound up playing 'strip' *Mortal-Kombat*, though aside from roaming hands and wandering tongues, we haven't gone all the way yet.

He's cute in not wanting to hurry. I love that he loves simply being with me.

Lawrence is doing much better, he came out of his fog Wednesday on a lower dose of pain meds and could carry on a coherent conversation. Talk about awkward? He commented about the hot young nurse who'd visited him and how if he'd been twenty years younger, he'd have put the moves on her. Yeah... No, I didn't tell him it was me. I did tell him I found Eaves, but startled him into messing up a portal spell and he... burst.

Much to my surprise, Lawrence doesn't want to retire right away, but he's going to be on medical leave for a while longer. Looks like I might wind up being an assistant investigator again, but really, I'm happy just being a plain ol' firefighter. I'll still help out if they ask, but my heart is pulling me into the flames.

Jason's stuck on the swing today, so he's gotta be at his station tomorrow as well. Next weekend is my turn. Groan. We might get together later, but I'm not going to let him stay up past his bedtime again. Three nights in a row is going to leave him in no shape to be of use to anyone in an emergency situation.

After a while, I get up and walk naked to the kitchen for a bowl of cereal. Once I polish it off and wash the bowl, I debate clothes. If I wear something, I have to wash it. Ultimately, I decide on a knee-length 'sleeping tee.' No plans to go out, so today equals comfort.

There's nothing on TV I want to watch this early on a Saturday, so I flip over to the PS4. I'm clicking back and forth between two games, trying to decide which one to pick back up when a flash of golden radiance from my balcony sets me on edge.

Laniah steps out of the cloud of light, brilliant, white feathery wings folding up behind her like the paintings you always see of angels. Only, her wings are quite a bit bigger by comparison. Physics, right? They're on par with mine for size, about half her height up to the bend, and a foot or two longer than her height from there to the tip.

My patio door clicks and opens on its own. She steps in.

"Hi."

"Come in," I deadpan.

As her wings become pure light and shrink into her back, her little porno-toga shifts color and grows into a pink sweater and jeans, though she remains barefoot. Wow. That's a neat trick. Maybe Natalie can enchant me some clothing that can survive shapeshifting. Not that I mind nudity, but it gets everyone around me uncomfortable and brings on undue attention.

She sits on the sofa beside me, at the edge like a nervous fourteen-year-old in her boyfriend's bedroom for the first time. "I wanted to talk to you."

I don't bother sitting up from a slouch so deep a midget walking by could see straight up my shirt. "Okay. Want some iced tea or something?"

"No, thanks." She smiles. "I don't want to bother you that long. It's about your mother."

"What?" I shoot upright, staring at her. "What about Mom?"

Laniah puts her hand on my knee, her expression comforting. "She is fine. I'm talking about the past."

"Oh." I relax—a little.

Like Daniel Graf, Laniah is not giving me any feeling of intent, other than by body language. If 'innocent' had a picture, she'd be it. Still though, I find myself not quite trusting her all the way.

"Your mother sought out your father under the influence of magic. Someone else—neither of your parents—wanted you to exist."

"How do you know that?" I ask. "Where's this coming from?"

"I'm an Elestari." Laniah makes a satisfied face as if that simple statement ought to explain everything.

"Right." I roll my eyes. "Okay, I'll bite. Why do they want me?"

"There's numerous reasons, but the one I, and others who think like me, fear the most is that you are the key to destroying the Armistice. There are groups within both the Elestari and Shaar'Nath who want the war to resume. As long as the mortal world exists, they are held back from slaughtering each other."

I fidget. "Graf almost cut my head off the other day. If they're so bent on killing each other, why not meet for duels here?"

"Because, it's small. A few at a time, and if our kind are destroyed here, it's only a nuisance. Our energy reforms in our home realm, though it can be human decades before we return. To us, it doesn't feel like any time has passed. Only if they slay each other in our realms is death true." She stares at me with such sadness in her eyes, I almost want to hug her and say it'll be okay.

Almost.

"Great. No pressure. What am I supposed to do?"

Laniah's innocence hardens and she stares into my eyes. "What is your intention toward the mortal world?"

"It's my home. I'm not going to burn down my house." I raise a finger. "I didn't burn down the last one. There was a drug lab a few trailers over."

Her sweetness returns with a broad smile. "Then you should worry only about being the woman your mother raised you to be for now." Laniah stands. "If you need help, you will have it."

"Uhh, thanks."

She walks to the patio. Her toga and wings return, and she zips off into the sky like someone shot her out of a huge crossbow. I can't help but feel jealous at her flight. Something tells me the Elestari *are* better in the air than us. Mom would say be happy I can fly at all. Most people can't.

Before I can grab the controller again, the phone rings. Sigh.

I trudge to my bedroom and grab it off the desk. "Hello?"

"Miss Amari?" asks a man with a Spanish accent.

"Who wants to know?" I ask in Spanish.

He laughs. "My name is Ernesto. I believe you are at least partially familiar with me."

"Yeah, some mage who blew himself up seemed to be pretty scared of you. Is your breath really that strong?"

Again, he laughs, though it's taken a patronizing, insulted tone. "It would be wise of you to back away from matters concerning Rossellini's restaurant."

"Oh. Whee. I guess I'm important if the Mob's threatening me. Look, man. There's nothing to back off on. For one thing, I'm not a cop. I'm with the fire department. Two, as far as I know, there's no evidence to go anywhere with. If anyone needs to be told to back off, it's the police or the DA. I'm not involved anymore."

"Hmm." Ernesto taps the phone for a few seconds. "You seem to have rather interesting skills. We may be in touch."

He hangs up.

Don't hold your breath.

After returning to the couch by way of the bathroom, I spend a minute staring at the controller, knowing the instant I touch it, some other interruption is going to land in my lap. Sure enough, a minute later when I click on *Fractured: The Endless Waste* (I do love a good post-apocalyptic game), my doorbell rings.

I jam one of the little sofa pillows in my mouth and bite it to muffle my growl of frustration.

Sorry little guy. I spit the pillow out, pause the game (which had only just loaded), and pad over to the door, ripping it open a little too hard.

Tracy and Ashley are standing outside. Tracey in her Starbucks uniform, Ashley in a bright yellow dress and pink flip-flops.

"Uhh, hi," I say.

"I'm sorry to bother you, but I got called in and... I can't find anyone to watch Ashley. Is there any chance she could stay with you for a couple hours?" Tracy stares at my chest the whole time, but not because of tits. She's dodging eye contact.

"Please?" asks Ashley with a huge smile.

"I'm being watched by angels who don't trust me, a mage's guild is probably hunting me, and I think the Mob's pissed off at me."

"Cool!" yells Ashley.

Tracy bites her lip. "It's all right. I'll find someone—"

"Naw. It's cool. Just letting you know. I can keep an eye on her."

"Wow, really?" Tracy's head pops up. She looks shocked, but smiles. "Oh, thanks! You're a lifesaver."

Ashley jumps in and hugs me.

"Sure, no problem. I wouldn't be a firefighter if I didn't want to help people." I pat the kid on the head.

"You're awesome." Tracy grins. "You have my number, right? I'm on the hook 'til five, but they might ask me to stay 'til eight. It's cool if you wanna bring her somewhere, just shoot me a text or something."

"All right, and yeah, I still have your number."

Tracy takes a knee, tells Ashley to behave herself, that she loves her, and she'll back soon. Once she trudges off, I ease the door closed. Well, so much for *Fractured*. That game's not for kids. We flop on the couch and I pull up a child-friendly adventure game with co-op play.

A few minutes of jumping over little red jellys with eyes and fanged fuzzballs later, Ashley asks, "Are you really a demon?"

"It's complicated."

She scrunches up her face. "That's what Mom said when I asked why she didn't tell Frank to beat it."

My character gets stuck in a slime trap, so I mash buttons as fast as I can to break free. "I'm kinda a demon but not really. Maybe I'm a half-demon."

"It's okay," says Ashley. "Mom says stair-types are bad. If you were bad, you wouldn't have killed Frank to protect me."

Her remark catches me off guard and I wind up mistiming a jump and falling to my pixelated death. I bite my lip, staring at the controller dangling in my fingers between my knees. "You saw that?"

Ashley pauses the game and gives me the most precious, serious look I've ever seen on an eight-year-old. "Only a little. But you threw him outta window, and he don't have wings." She grins. "It's okay. He deserved it."

"Yeah. Guess he did." I flick my nail at the controller for a few seconds. "A man tried to hurt me like that when I was a little older than you."

"Was he dating your mom, too?" Ashley digs her toes into the carpet.

I shake my head. "No. He tried to get me to go in his car."

She gasps. "You didn't!"

"No. I'm still here, right?"

"Whew!" Ashley fake-wipes her forehead. "He would'a taken you away and you'd never be back."

"You're probably right."

She smiles. "Did you kill him?"

I laugh, caught off guard again. "No, my father did."

Her eyes widen so much I feel guilty. "Is *he* the demon? Or is your Mom?"

"Dad."

"Your mom's normal, right?"

"Yeah, a lesser mage. But we're not really demons. We just kinda look like them. Demons are made up."

She ponders for a little while, staring at her controller while her eyebrows do tricks. Eventually, she looks up at me with disappointment on her face. "Does that mean you can't teach me black magic?"

"Hah!" I giggle. "I don't know any black magic… and even if I did, I couldn't teach you. Don't let fear open you to darkness. It's not strength. It's weakness. Fear only causes more fear."

"Ugh." Ashley rolls her eyes. "Great. I summoned the lamest demon."

"Who are you calling lame?" I tickle her sides, laughing.

She squeals, trying to squirm away. A few minutes later, she wails, "Stop," so I let her breathe. Giggles and laughter continue for a little while before we get quiet and serious again.

When the silence gets awkward we, resume playing.

"I still think you're a lame demon," says Ashley. "Guess I shouldn't have used strawberry syrup instead of blood to draw the star."

I throw a sofa pillow, bouncing it off her head. "No ritual magic until you're at least eighteen."

"Aww, but Brooklyn!" she fake-whines.

"No buts. I mean it. Besides. You have to be eighteen to sign a binding contract, even with the powers of darkness."

She stares up at me with a 'really!' face. It takes all I have to keep myself from laughing. "Yeah. You don't need to be afraid anymore. You were scared with that man around, and you had every right to be. I think you still are."

Ashley leans against me. "Yeah."

"My mom didn't have a lot of money when I was a kid either. I know how it is." I put an arm around her. "Hey, I got your back. 'Kay?"

She raises her head and smiles. "Okay."

I sigh. Guess the kid's got herself a pet demon.

Well, good for her.

Brooklyn's story continues in Book 2 - The Shadow Collector.

Brooklyn thought nothing would ever surprise her again after learning her father is an extraplanar being—until the police ask her for help.

For most of her life, the cops have been a thorn in her side, always in the way of a good time. By seventeen, she'd spent more time in police cars than some rookies. With age comes (a little) restraint, and she's managed to avoid getting in trouble for six whole years. Working for the Philadelphia Fire Department offers a sense of belonging and purpose she never had growing up, even if the whole 'adulting' thing sucks.

After responding to a fire call eerily similar to the one that claimed her childhood home, a local detective seeks her out. He's hunting a serial killer who preys on the city's homeless, taking the lives of those no one cares to see. Every victim's body has so far been stolen from the morgue, frustrating the investigation to the point he's willing to rely on a psychic—even a former delinquent.

Brooklyn senses a connection between the recent fire, the murders, and a mysteriously guilty little girl, but her respect for the law only goes so far.

ACKNOWLEDGMENTS

Thank you for reading The Shadow Collector!

Additional thanks to Alexandria Thompson for the cover and interior art!

ABOUT THE AUTHOR

Originally from South Amboy NJ, Matthew has been creating science fiction and fantasy worlds for most of his reasoning life. Since 1996, he has developed the "Divergent Fates" world, in which *Division Zero, Virtual Immortality, The Awakened Series, The Harmony Paradox, and the Daughter of Mars series* take place. Along with being an editor at Curiosity Quills press, he has worked in IT and technical support.

Matthew is an avid gamer, a recovered WoW addict, Gamemaster for two custom RPG systems, and a fan of anime, British humour, and intellectual science fiction that questions the nature of reality, life, and what happens after it.

He is also fond of cats.

Visit me online at:
Facebook: https://www.facebook.com/MatthewSCoxAuthor
Amazon: https://www.amazon.com/author/mscox
Pinterest: https://www.pinterest.com/matthewcox10420/
Goodreads: https://www.goodreads.com/author/show/7712730.Matthew_S_Cox
Email: mcox2112@gmail.com

OTHER BOOKS BY MATTHEW S. COX

Divergent Fates Universe Novels

Division Zero series

- Division Zero
- Lex De Mortuis
- Thrall
- Guardian
- Harbinger

The Awakened series

- Prophet of the Badlands
- Archon's Queen
- Grey Ronin
- Daughter of Ash
- Zero Rogue
- Angel Descended

Daughter of Mars series

- The Hand of Raziel
- Araphel
- Ghost Black

Virtual Immortality series

- Virtual Immortality
- The Harmony Paradox

Divergent Fates Anthology

(Fiction Novels - Adult)

The Roadhouse Chronicles Series

- One More Run
- The Redeemed
- Dead Man's Number

Faded Skies series

- Heir Ascendant
- Ascendant Unrest
- Ascendant Revolution

Temporal Armistice Series

- Nascent Shadow
- The Shadow Collector
- The Gate to Oblivion

Vampire Innocent series

- A Nighttime of Forever
- A Beginner's Guide to Fangs
- The Artist of Ruin
- The Last Family Road Trip
- The Phantom Oracle

Standalones

- Wayfarer: AV494
- Axillon99
- Chiaroscuro: The Mouse and the Candle
- The Spirits of Six Minstrel Run

- The Far Side of Promise anthology
- Operation: Chimera (with Tony Healey)
- The Dysfunctional Conspiracy (with Christopher Veltmann)

Winter Solstice series (with J.R. Rain)

- Convergence
- Containment
- Catalyst

Alexis Silver series (with J.R. Rain)

- Silver Light
- Deep Silver
- Silver Quarrel

Samantha Moon Origins series (with J.R. Rain)

- New Moon Rising
- Moon Mourning

Vampire For Hire series (with J.R. Rain)

- Moon Master
- Dead Moon

Maddy Wimsey series (with J.R. Rain)

- The Devil's Eye
- The Drifting Gloom

Samantha Moon Case Files series (with J.R. Rain)

- Blood Moon

Immortal Operative series (with J.R. Rain)

- Broken Ice

Young Adult Novels

The Eldritch Heart Series

- The Eldritch Heart
- The Cursed Crown

Evergreen Series

- Evergreen
- The World That Remains

Standalones

- Caller 107
- The Summer the World Ended
- Nine Candles of Deepest Black
- The Forest Beyond the Earth
- Out of Sight
- Evergreen

Middle Grade Novels

Tales of Widowswood series

- Emma and the Banderwigh
- Emma and the Silk Thieves
- Emma and the Silverbell Faeries

- Emma and the Elixir of Madness
- Emma and the Weeping Spirit

Standalones

- Citadel: The Concordant Sequence
- The Cursed Codex
- The Menagerie of Jenkins Bailey
- Sophie's Light